# Free From The Living Dead End

Miguel Figueroa Manners

# Index

# Chapter 1: My Wish Came True

Date: 9/3/26

Hey, if you're reading this, I'm probably dead... or worse. I never liked writing, but when it's the end of the world, you have a lot of time on your hands. If you never went outside in these trying times, you wouldn't know that there's a zombie apocalypse. I don't know how, what, when, or why, but all I know is that it happened, and for some reason, I'm happy that it did.

I know that sounds crazy considering a virus is making people eat each other alive, but I finally feel free to do my own thing! I can finally do anything I want and not have a care in the world! Everything's free, no more chores, I can go wherever I want. It feels amazing! So far it's been 8 days since the zombies flooded into my town and a lot has happened.

7 Days ago: It felt like Covid-19 all over again. The government telling us there's a new virus, wear a mask, and to quarantine. While I was quarantined, my sister called and told me to watch the news. A popular subject was cannibalism happening in a big Asian city. Then it spread to Europe and eventually made its way to the US in only two weeks.

6 days ago: The government told everyone to barricade our doors and windows and to stock up on supplies. This freaked everyone out more than they already were, including me. I barricaded my house the best I could with supplies from Home Depot.

5 Days ago: everything was quiet, no people, no kids playing outside, some cars here and there but not nearly as much as before. I spent most of my time watching the news or playing video games.

4 Days ago: Hell, zombies started to flood into town full on SPRINTING! I hoped for only walking zombies, not SPRINTING zombies. I peeked through the wood

protecting my house and there was CHAOS. People screaming, shooting, running. There were countless zombies everywhere running in all directions.

BANG, a loud sound erupted from the front of my house. I let out a  yelp in return. I wished I didn't do that because zombies started to pound the windows and doors of my house. I could hear windows cracking, the wood from the doors snapping.

The barricade of wood planks being the only thing keeping the zombies outside, I was worried they would break eventually. The banging got louder and I grabbed my pocket knife off the kitchen counter and ran to the bathroom.

3 days ago: I couldn't sleep, not after what happened. I hid inside my bathroom. With my pocket knife firmly in hand. Never taking my eyes off the door. The banging stopped a few hours ago but I was still in shock. My heart was practically beating out of my chest.

After what felt like hours, I finally found the balls to stand up and walk to the bathroom door. I stayed there contemplating if I should open it. I held my pocket knife ready to attack any zombie I saw.

I placed my hand on the door handle and swung it open. I jumped forward ready to attack and... nothing, no zombies. I heaved a massive sigh of relief, short lived because I looked at the state of my house.

There were holes all over the walls, I looked down and saw BLOOD seeping through them. I guess when it's the zombie apocalypse that just becomes the norm.

I started to walk around my house. A lot of the holes weren't big enough for a person to walk through but big enough that it worried me. So to fix this, I went to my junkdrawer, got a lot of duct tape, and went to work.

...

It wasn't much but it should do the job. After all that I realized that I was exhausted from getting no sleep. I decided after I fixed the house a little bit more, I would go to bed.

2 days ago: Putting up the wood planks and sealing it up with duct tape made it almost impossible to see outside. I expected it to be loud in the end of the world, but for the most part, it's surprisingly quiet. Sure a few screams here and there, maybe some gunshots, but that's mostly it. I have a couple of food items but I don't know how long they'll last.

1 day ago: I woke up feeling great. I started my day off humming and making myself a peanut butter and honey sandwich. Then, I grabbed a glass of milk that was still in the fridge. The power still worked, so later I got in my chair, turned on my xbox and started to play videogames offline. I made sure to keep the volume extra quiet. I didn't want to attract anymore zombies like I did before.

While I was playing I ate so many snacks my stomach started to hurt. I started to doze off after a couple of hours playing video games so I turned off my xbox and headed to bed.

Today: I woke up ready to eat. So I opened up the fridge and to my disappointment, all I saw was pickles. "I'm *not* eating that," I said with a stern voice, and I meant it. I figured if I wanted to fix my issue. I would have to go outside.

So I put on my black pants, slipped on my black socks, tied my black steel toe tactical boots, put on my white shirt, and zipped up my plain black jacket. Can you guess what my favorite color is? Also, I would be stupid if I didn't bring a weapon. I've been waiting for a zombie apocalypse to happen for quite some time now, so I have a few.

I have 2 throwing axes that I got from my dad. They are black with a razor sharp blade, and on the butt of the ax, there's a spike. It has a long handle but short enough I can use one in each hand. They both have sheaths that attach to a belt supported by velcro.

I also have a black machete. I got it as a prize for winning a game of bingo a week before Christmas. It has a rubber handle with a small piece of rope that wraps around your wrists and a long flexible blade. Like the axes, it also has a sheath that can be attached to a belt that's supported with velcro.

Along with those, I have a white katana that I got from a garage sale, surprisingly cheap at only 30$. It looks like a normal katana, but completely white.

It took a bit of contemplating, but I finally picked the coolest one. I ended up going with the 2 throwing axes as my main weapons. I attached the sheaths to my belt, and placed the axes against both hips. Then, when I was ready. I walked to the living room.

I grabbed a hammer to unnail the planks that were blocking the door. After about 5 minutes, I finally detached the planks. I unsheathed one of my axes ready to attack if there were any zombies. I slowly opened the door, and to be honest... things could be worse.

# Chapter 2: Window Shopping

Date: 9/11/26

I slowly opened the door and it was so bright it hurt my eyes, but eventually they readjusted. I was shocked at what I saw. The kind of things you only see in the movies. Never thought I would see anything like this in real life. I saw blood trails, a few zombies limping around, debris everywhere, and trashed up houses.

*Things could be worse,* I thought to myself. My goal is to find food at a nearby supermarket and maybe get my first zombie kill. Should be pretty easy considering I have 2 axes.

I eventually opened the second part of my door, walked outside and finally got to breathe fresh air again. To think, I was in that house for about 4 days...

I stepped out into the street, looked back at my house and it's... well destroyed. Holes and some blood splatter for finishing touches. *It looks a lot worse from the outside.* I looked around and some of the neighbors' houses looked similar to mine. Though some were untouched. I'm surprised mine is still standing after all this. *Well, it is what it is.*

I continue down the street and I see a zombie further down the block. *Ok, this is it,* I think while walking towards the zombie. I unsheath both my axes waiting for the zombie to turn around to see me. It had a blue shirt with brown pants matched with black shoes and... he's just standing there, head down doing nothing. I was staring at him longer than I should, so I decided to get his attention.

I called out, "Hey over here!"

He turned his head and looked me dead in the face. I got in my fighting stance ready for him to start sprinting at me, but all he did was wobble in my direction. *What!?* I thought they were sprinters, not walkers! He started to bring up his arms to attack, but I'd simply just back up a few feet. *I thought the zombies were only sprinters?* After a minute of me stepping back every time he tried to attack me, I got bored and didn't want to kill him anymore.

After quietly jogging away from the zombie. I had to cut through a small neighborhood to reach the supermarket. I remembered my friend used to live in this neighborhood. So I decided to pay him a visit.

...

It took longer than I expected, around 20 minutes. I had to sneak past over a dozen zombies. Luckily, I was only seen by that one slow zombie. I had to turn just one more street to make it to my friend Tanner's house. I turned a corner and saw his house in the distance.

I started to get nervous. *What if he was hurt? What if he wasn't there? What if he was... dead?* I started to get goosebumps, trying to convince myself that he was in his house drinking Dr Pepper and playing video games, because that's what he normally does.

I stood staring, wanting him to come out, but he never did. I studied his house and it looked destroyed. It wasn't boarded up, the windows were shattered and the door was opened. This was the first time I was kinda sad in a while. I didn't even want to go in. I was worried if he wasn't there, or worse... he WAS in there. I didn't want to find out so I left. *Get used to it! The zombie apocalypse isn't for everyone. Cheer up. You've dreamed of this.*

I started to get back on the path to the supermarket and I saw a sprinting zombie with a hood and a backpack, running in my direction fast. I readyed my axes to attack. It noticed me and slowed down to a halt. I looked at the sprinter closer and realized it wasn't a zombie! It was a PERSON! A REAL, LIVING PERSON!

Before I could greet him I looked behind him, and saw that he was being chased by 2 sprinting zombies. They were about 50 ft away but they were closing in at an alarming rate.

I waited for the first zombie to get close enough. When it did I brought up the ax in my right hand and SLAMMED it as hard as I could through his head. It made a massive crack sound then a slurring, swishing. I yanked my axe out of the zombie's head.

Then the other sprinter tackled me out of the blue. I dropped both my axes by how much force it hit me with. *Damn this zombie is strong.* I looked up and saw that the zombie and I were face to face. It lunged, trying to bite me, but I kept a firm hand on his forehead so it couldn't.

FINALLY the ALIVE person decided to help me after what felt like an eternity of fighting this zombie on the ground. He kicked him off of me with his shoe, and it landed on its back. After that I got on top of it, picked up one of my axes and drove it through its head. I flinched from the nasty warm blood that squirted from his head onto my face.

I stood up, looked the person and said "You couldn't have helped sooner!?"

There was a pause before the person responded, "Miguel?"

My heart dropped. How does he know my name? He took off his hoodie and I got a clear look at his face.

"Tanner?" I said in disbelief.

"It's me," Tanner said with a grin.

I ran up to him and hugged him. This was the first time I ever hugged him in my life. I didn't want to make it weird so I stopped after 2 seconds.

I was practically jumping on my feet, "How are you alive? I saw your house and it was a complete wreck!"

Tanner responded coldly, "Does it matter how I survived?"

"No but-"

"Then I don't have to answer."

...

*Rude.*

After a long awkward pause Tanner said, "Oh yeah, I have something for you."

While he was saying that, he took off his backpack and he revealed a sad deflated backpack he was also wearing behind his back.

"It's some military backpack. I was kinda just saving one in case I found a use for it and here we are. You... backpackless" Tanner smirked.

"Alright bruh no need to shame me, but thanks for the backpack anyway," I said jokingly. I remembered why I was out here in the first place, "Want to come window shopping with me for a bit?"

Tanner scoffed. "Sure, just take a shower. The zombies can probably smell the blood off you a mile away."

"Blood? Where?"

For context, Tanner is a good friend from school. I met him in 4th grade and we have stayed friends ever since. He has wavy black hair that goes down to his neck, dark brown eyes, he's skinny, and fast on his feet. Personality wise, he's a pretty calm dude, smart, quick with jokes too. Tanner and I were in our sophomore years of high school before the zombie apocalypse happened. A month before his birthday. Tanner and I are pretty similar but I have dark brown curly hair, freckles, and an obsession over the zombie apocalypse.

After talking for a bit, Tanner and I go inside the first house that looks clean.

I shout, "DIBS! I CALL TAKING A SHOWER FIRST!"

Tanner grabbed my shoulder before I could run off, "*Shut up*, the zombies will hear you."

"oh yeah, sorry."

We closed the door behind us and walked into the living room. We searched every room for zombies and thankfully we didn't find any. We put our bags on the living room floor and I headed toward the bathroom. I turned on the light and was excited to take a shower.

I looked in the mirror and saw all the semi-dry blood smeared across my face. It felt nasty and sticky but at least I looked kinda cool. The one thing I was worried about is if I would get infected by the blood on my skin.

I didn't want to test it out, so I took a hot shower and washed all the blood off as quickly as I could. After I was clean, I put my clothes back on and headed back to the living room.

I saw Tanner looking through all the cabinets and he said, "They must have moved away or something, there's nothing here." I looked at him and he knew it was his turn to take a shower.

After 5 minutes Tanner got out of the shower and had a sour expression on his face. "You used all the HOT WATER."

"Sorry about that, forgot to tell you," I said while trying not to laugh.

Tanner said with an annoyed tone, "Next time you need help with a zombie, I'm gonna take my sweet time."

After that we finally went back outside and started to head in the direction of the supermarket.

I asked "why didn't you kill the zombie that was on top of me before, don't you have a weapon?"

"Yes I have a weapon... I have a knife."

Confused, I said, "then why didn't you use it?"

"I don't know, I thought you liked killing things so I let you have it."

I couldn't tell if he was joking or serious. "What are you talking about? You can still-"

Tanner stopped walking and turned his head to me, "I was scared... I was caught up in the moment, I didn't know what to do. I was running from people that wanted to *actually* eat me alive! I don't know how you can dream about living in an apocalypse like this, or how you can kill someone so easily without a second thought."

*Kill someone? I'm not killing someone am I? I mean they're zombies that eat people, that's far from human. Or what if they're the type of zombies that are still alive but can't help themselves? Is it still wrong to kill them?*

After a long awkward pause of just walking, we finally see the supermarket.

"Finally, we're here" I said, breaking the awkward silence.

Surprisingly there weren't many zombies while we were traveling to the supermarket. I had a bad feeling about the whole thing but I never said it out loud. We walked onto the parking lot and I could tell Tanner was scared by the way he looked at the supermarket. To be honest, I was a little worried too.

The parking lot was completely empty except for 2 cars at the front, which means we had NO cover. To make it worse, there was a group of zombies on the very right side of the market. They were far enough I don't think they would have seen us, but I wasn't taking chances. I put my arms loose to the side, opened my mouth and walked with a limp toward the entrance.

"Meerrrrrrr," I groaned.

Tanner looked at me in disgust while keeping up with me, "Miguel... what the hell are you doing?"

I whispered, "I'm blending in"

"Blending in as what... are you trying to act like a zombie?"

"Maybe," I said before getting back into character, "Merrrr"

"Maybe you're just, stupid?"

I stopped walking in the middle of the parking lot and turned to face Tanner, "Would you rather make it to the market *without* killing a zombie OR try to kill a horde and *die* the first day into the apocalypse."

Tanner Looked at me conflicted, "Whatever."

I got back into character and Tanner was limping beside me with his arms out in front like a chicken.

"Meeerrr" I groaned.

Tanner huffed, "We're already here. You can stop with the act."

*Oh,* I was too focused on my zombie impression. I didn't realize we made it to the front door. Even more, zombies didn't spot us, I guess theatre class really paid off. I looked at the sliding glass door, it was dark and quiet.

Before we entered I asked Tanner, "What do you want from the supermarket?"

Tanner replied with "Food dumbass, that's why it's a supermarket, you know... a place to buy food."

"Calm down dude, you're 3 for 3 for acting like a douche today."

I walked forward– POP! I jumped from the sudden noise. The sound of the sliding door opening echoed in the empty area. After Tanner laughed at my reaction, we entered the store. I took out one of my axes and held it with both hands. It was so quiet. I could hear my own heart beat. I walked in half expecting to die by a zombie surprise attack. Then suddenly, the lights turned on. I jumped then turned my head back and saw Tanner next to a light switch.

Tanner smirked, "For someone who likes the zombie apocalypse, you sure get scared easy"

We looked at the store then looked at each other. Then realization hit us like a bus. *We can have whatever we want!* Admittedly we went to the candy aisle... and to our surprise there wasn't much. Half of the shelves were empty and all the good candy was gone. The little candy that was left was the type grandmas would eat. Coconut and chocolate, hard carmel. Sugar cookies. Though I still filled my bag up with it and shoveled most of it in my mouth.

Then we explored and found a ping pong table box in the athletic section. I opened it with my ax and set it up while Tanner helped. It was a close couple of matches but of course I won 3 out of the 4 games we played.

Then we went into the game aisle and found a really nice chess board. We set up the board in the middle of the aisle, and played another tournament (chess edition), but this wasn't even a close game at all. I won 1 out of the 5 games we played. Tanner says I didn't win a single game, because I counted the time we had a draw, as a win for me, but haters gonna hate. We also played checkers with the same board.

After checkers, we decided to play tag in the supermarket and it was as fun as I had imagined. Running aisle through aisle, throwing random stuff at each other. It was all fun and games until I was looking at Tanner behind me and hit my ribs on a counter.

Tanner ran up behind me, "Miguel? Are you ok?"

I said while bent over and wheezing, "yep yep im good... just give me a sec."

While I was getting my breath back, I looked at the counter and saw it was a gun case. Full of stuff. Rifles, pistols, crossbows and more.

Tanner was wide eyed and asked, "can we get one of them?"

I'm skeptical, "sure just... not right now, maybe when we leave the supermarket we can both pick one up"

With a disappointed tone Tanner replied with "Ok."

After playing tag, we were both tired. So to rest up, we went to the camping section and got one of the five person tents off the shelf. We also made sure to grab two sleeping bags so we could spend the night comfortably.

After we got half (if you could even call it that) of the tent complete, I was curious what time it was. I walked a little bit away to see the sliding doors across the store. It was still bright outside, but after all that messing around and fighting those zombies, we were tired. I walked back to the half made tent, and saw Tanner squatting at the completed part of it scratching his head.

Tanner sighed looking back at me, "This manual doesn't make any sense. We're probably just gonna sleep outside the tent tonight."

"That's fine with me, but maybe we just need a little break, then we can start working on it again."

"Alright," Tanner paused, "I'm gonna go to the soda aisle, do you want anything?"

"I don't like soda that much. Do you want me to come with you?"

Tanner shook his head, "No I got it."

With that Tanner turned around and walked away. Now I'm laying down on the floor and I started to think about everything. *How did Tanner live through the wave of zombies that wrecked our town? His house was absolutely destroyed, blood, broken windows, door wide open. How is he still alive? Is his family alive?*

I started to doze off but suddenly the store ALARM goes off. It sounded like a school fire alarm screaming in my ears. I sprung up off the ground. *Where's Tanner?* I ran over to the soda aisle as fast as I could. I looked around, but Tanner wasn't there! He was GONE! I felt my eyes go wide. *He has to be somewhere,* I said to myself. Before I thought things couldn't get worse. My heart dropped, POP!

I ran over to the edge of one of the aisles, peaking my head over. The sliding door was wide open and zombies were pouring in. At least a dozen or more.

The zombies were looking all over the place, like they're trying to pinpoint the source of the noise, but they couldn't, because the siren sounded like it was everywhere in the store. They started to spread out. *Maybe I can kill them one by one,* I thought as I took out one of my axes.

I saw a zombie alone in an aisle looking away and straight up at the ceiling. I slowly came up behind it, and while I was getting closer. I brought my ax behind my back more and more. Then slammed it into the zombie's head. The crack of the zombie's skull was silenced by the blaring alarm. The zombie started to fall on the ground but I grabbed its waist and gently placed it on the ground so I wouldn't make too much noise.

My main goal was to find Tanner, get the hell out of here and hopefully stop the alarm. I looked at the main entrance and thankfully, I saw multiple zombies stuck trying to get through the sliding doors. I started to walk across the store, looking down every aisle, and to my luck, I saw a group of zombies in the middle of aisle three.

The closest one spotted me. I prayed that the zombie was a walker, but as luck would have it, it started to sprint towards me. I got ready to attack, but in the corner of my eye I saw a massive figure run at me from the right. When I noticed it, I hopped back as quickly as I could. The figure collided with the zombie that was running at me. I heard a massive crack as both of them went flying to the left.

Only one of the two zombies got up. The other laid lifeless on the floor. The bigger zombie picked itself up and turned around. It was over 10 meters away, but I could tell the zombie towered over me. For being tall, surprisingly it had a beer gut, but the most noticeable feature was one of its arms was ripped clean off from the sleeve. Worse, the zombie's other arm was stained in blood.

This massive dead-dude got up immediately and started to sprint at me, then lunged. Right before it could grab me, I jumped to the left and I watched him fall to the ground. *This is my chance.* I brought my ax over my head and rammed the butt of it right through the zombie's side

I tried to pull out my ax but it wouldn't budge. I put my foot on his back and pulled with two hands. First it was slow but then my whole body sprang backwards. *Oof!* I fell on my butt and dropped my weapon. I looked for my ax on the floor. It was out of arms reach. I took a piece of the zombie's side out and blood started to pour from the wound.

The zombie turned its massive body and started to crawl towards me. It was falling over itself trying to crawl with one arm. I scooted frantically across the floor trying to get away. Suddenly, the zombie fell one last time and stopped moving in a pool of his own blood.

For a few seconds I sat in pure shock. I saw liquid hit the bottom of my shoe. I tilt my head to the right and see the zombie's blood slowly moving, touching the sole of my foot. Gross, I immediately stood up.

I kept getting distracted, *where's Tanner?* I sneaked aisle through aisle, trying not to be seen by the increasing amount of zombies. Before long, I spotted the gun counter. *Maybe when the alarm went off, Tanner went to go get a weapon.*

I walked slowly toward it and spotted shattered glass all over the floor. I looked inside the case and I saw one of the pistols gone. An M1911. I walked behind the counter and before I knew it, I watched Tanner sitting on the floor, raising a gun to my head.

*Click*

He **pulled** the **trigger**.

I closed my eyes, prepared to get shot, but... nothing happened, No loud bang, just a click from the gun.

I opened my eyes and Tanner started sobbing. Before I could say anything Tanner threw the gun at my head. The butt end hit my eye.

My head cocked back and I yelled, "Ow! What the hell! I could have lost an eye!"

While I was holding my eye I got slammed to the ground. I put my arms over my head trying to shield myself.

Tanner yelled while hitting me, "Die! die! die! zombie bastard!"

I grab his right arm, "TANNER STOP! It's me!"

Tanner studies my face, "Miguel?"

"Yes It's me!" I yelled.

Tanner stared at me for a moment then wiped his teary eyes. "I'm sorry" He repeated while standing up.

I stayed on the ground waiting for Tanner to pick me up, but he just walked past me, still repeating "I'm sorry." *Hits me then doesn't even look at me. Thanks a lot bro.* I jogged to catch up with Tanner.

I grabbed Tanner's shoulder and said, "Follow me. I know a path."

I took the lead while crouching to keep myself low. Tanner followed behind. I followed the trail of dead bodies back to the store entrance... and it didn't look good.

Massive groups of zombies were around the entrance and across the store. *We gotta think of something.*

Tanner tapped my shoulder, seemingly out of his tear-filled daze, "Miguel, Zombies are attracted to light right?"

"In like all zombie movies they are, " I said.

"I think I saw flood lights in the camping section."

My eyes went wide, "Holy, dude you're a genius! Let's do it."

...

The alarms were so loud they were giving me a headache. We made it to the camping section and it was practically empty except for a few camping tents and a couple of boxes. Tanner and I ran to one of them and saw that it was a battery-powered flood light. Tanner ripped it open with his knife. He clicked the power button but... nothing happened. The light didn't turn on.

"What the hell!" Tanner yelled.

I grabbed it from his hands, "Give me that."

I looked at the light to see if anything was wrong. I grabbed the bottom of it and popped off a cap. The battery compartment was completely empty.

"Batteries not included."

Tanner's lips twitched and he put his hands on his head, "What are we gonna do then! There's nothing we can do!"

I snapped back, "Calm down, we just need to find something else!"

I start looking through the shelves. The only other thing on the shelves is a couple of boxes of lighter fluid. I checked below. It was all dark and I could barely see. I tried to look closer and I saw a silhouette of a black box all the way in the back. I reached my arm and grabbed it, pulling it out and facing it to a light. It was an electric lighter.

*Useless.* I drop my arms thinking of what else I can do, my head facing down. I look at the shelves one more time, there's nothing except 2 bottles of lighter fluid and an electric lighter.

Lighter fluid? I look at the box in my hand.

"Tanner, I have an idea. Just trust me ok."

...

I couldn't believe Tanner went with my idea. We both grabbed a bottle of lighter fluid and made our way to the clothing section. We found the nearest circular clothing rack and started to drench it.

"Don't get this on you," I said while wetting the clothes.

Tanner called out, "I think that's enough fluid."

I put the bottle down and took the electric lighter out of the packaging and thank God, it was charged. I held the only button down and a purple spark formed at the tip. I aimed it under a dress and it caught a small flame that was spreading quickly. I went to the opposite side and started another flame. In no time at all the clothing rack was engulfed in flames. The mass groaning of the zombies was louder than the alarm as they started to recognize the fire.

Tanner slapped my chest with the back of his hand, "Common, We gotta go!"

We both took off in a sprint towards the entrance. We went the long way to the entrance to avoid the zombie hordes. One zombie was in the aisle we were running in. I grabbed his jacket and threw him into a wall of men's deodorant. All the other zombies were going towards the flames. Our plan was actually working!

The sliding doors were bent and broken from the zombies fighting to get through. Me and Tanner sprint through the doors and the biggest relief filled my mind.

I turn to the left to face Tanner, "We did it!" I yelled.

Even Tanner smiled while running away from the entrance. Before we could bask in the glory of our escape, I looked past Tanner and a line of zombies were pounding on the store walls. They heard us immediately and started branching off the wall sprinting towards us.

"SHIT! SHIT! KEEP RUNNING!" I screamed.

We ran as fast as we could, and soon enough, made it to a neighborhood. We sprinted down the street trying to lose the horde, but apparently that wasn't good enough. The zombies were relentless. Tanner called me over and we jumped a couple of fences. Then we had to run through some trees in different backyards until we lost the screaming. Still running, we made it to a street and I saw my house in the distance. It's like I was heading there subconsciously. We finally stopped running when I reached my house with no zombies in sight. We stood next to a tree, panting.

I asked, catching my breath, "Are they still following us?"

Tanner said bent over with his hands on his knees, "No, no they stopped, I don't see any."

Immediately after he said that, I threw up. Tanner looked at me and then at my puke, and then HE threw up. Then we puked together, And that was probably the best barf I ever had.

# Chapter 3: Brothers From Another Mother

After Tanner and I puked our guts out, Tanner took a breather and looked at my house. "Are you sure it's safe to live there? It's hanging by a thread."

I shrugged, "We're only gonna stay here for a little bit."

Words couldn't describe how tired we felt. We entered the house and it was a complete mess. The kitchen was overrun with plates, the carpet was unvacuumed and the duct tape I put up didn't help with the aesthetic.

"Sorry, I kind of forgot it was this dirty."

Holes, trash, blood... not an ideal place to live, but it should last for the meanwhile. I checked the time and it was 6:32 at night.

I was exhausted, "Hey, wanna head to bed?"

Tanner just nodded with his eyes half-closed and his hands on his head. I walked to my room, opened the door and saw that the floor was covered in clothes with half-eaten bags of chips and snacks. *Dang, I need to take care of myself more.*

I closed the door and walked back to Tanner, "Guess we're sleeping in the living room."

I laid a blanket and pillow on my living room floor while Tanner sat on my only couch.

"You sure you want me to take the couch?" Tanner questioned.

I said, "Nah it's fine, you're the guest."

At this point, I didn't care where I was sleeping. I was too exhausted.

I also felt bad for dragging Tanner to the supermarket with me. Letting him sleep on the couch was the least I could do. Right before I was about to fall asleep, Tanner suddenly said, "Can I tell you something?"

"Yeah sure."

"Remember when you asked me how I survived the first day?"

I stayed quiet and he continued.

"You know my mom, she's always watching the news. So, when she saw them talking about people turning into zombies, I told her it was just propaganda."

Tanner's voice started to shake, "I was in my room when mom started screaming from the kitchen. I ran downstairs and zombies were already banging on the door... my mom yelled at me to lock myself in my room. I didn't even argue, I ran up the stairs and locked my door, not long after..."

Tanner choked on his words.

I turned my head to see Tanner, his face was red with his tears soaking my couch.

Tanner took a deep shaky breath before he continued, "long story short... she died. After 2 days of hiding in my room, I went downstairs and didn't see her. Just my carpet stained with blood."

After Tanner finished his sentence, he let it all out, he cried and cried. I never thought I would see my friend cry, but there we were. Tanner turned over and cried into his pillow.

After a while of listening to his muffled cries, he suddenly stopped. I sat up and looked at Tanner's face, he was passed out drooling into the pillow. *I should probably sleep too.*

Date: 9/12/26

I woke up with sunlight shining through the cracks of the boarded windows. I checked on Tanner and he was staring up at the ceiling. I relaxed and placed my hands behind my head as I laid on the floor.

Tanner said, almost whispering, "You think we'll turn into zombies?"

I took a long pause to think, "No, we won't."

"Really? Just like that?"

"I will do everything in my power to make sure that doesn't happen. I will never let you turn into a zombie, I promise."

Tanner scoffed and stood up, "That's stupid... but I'll try to do the same." He then stood up and walked to the kitchen. I noticed he had a smile tugging on his face.

I closed my eyes again, still feeling tired. I almost fell back asleep, but after a while, suddenly I smelled smoke. I immediately got up off the floor, and ran into the kitchen worried that the house was burning down, but all I saw was Tanner surrounded by a cloud of smoke.

I yelled, "Tanner what are you doing!?"

"I'm cooking!" Tanner shouted.

Tanner took a pan over to the kitchen sink and turned on the faucet, the pan sizzled while smoke came out of it.

"Sorry about the pan," Tanner said while trying to scrape off black chunks from it.

I laughed, "What were you even trying to cook?

Tanner mumbled under his breath, "Cheese quesadillas"

I groaned, "Well, I'll just settle for the candy in my backpack for breakfast."

Tanner put the pan back on the stove, "I'm already making food just give me a second."

Not wanting to argue. I walked over to the table and sat down, trying to wake up. Tanner came by and handed me a plate of food. I look down and see a folded tortilla filled up with cheese. I take a bite. It is the most bland food I have tried in a while.

The quesadilla is soggy and even the cheese is bad. *How do you mess up cheese?* But in the moment, it wasn't the worst thing in the world. After all that running, I could eat anything. I scarfed down half the cheese tortilla.

I paused to ask Tanner, "Greg is probably still at his house. You wanna go see him?"

Tanner stopped what he was doing and turned his head to look at me, "He hasn't answered any of my texts or calls."

"Wait, you can still call people and stuff?"

"Yeah? It's not like cell service just dipped."

"Mmmm, I guess that's true, I don't have cell service because I forgot to pay for my phone thing this month."

Tanner tilted his head, "Your parents don't pay for stuff like that?"

"They do but... it's complicated. You want to go to Gregs?"

"Sure," Tanner then said under his breath, "hopefully he's not dead."

I was taken aback, "Woah, don't think like that. He's not dead. He's probably out looking for us right now".

Tanner sighed, "Maybe you're right."

I got a little mad at Tanner for even thinking Greg was dead. He can't be dead, right? He is the strongest person I know. I think he also wanted the zombie apocalypse to happen, so maybe he was prepared like me.

I stood up remembering that Tanner's birthday was coming up, "Hey, I got an early birthday present for you."

I ran to my room and grabbed my katana from the closet. I put the katana behind my back.

I walked back into the dining room, "For your birthday I was going to give you a $20 gift card but since the zombie apocalypse happened I don't think you'll need it. So, instead I'm gonna give you my katana!"

I held my white katana towards Tanner. I was hoping for a big reaction but Tanner just said, "You know my birthday is at the end of the month right?"

"Beggars can't be choosers." I barked back.

Tanner took the katana from my hands. I could see him try to suppress a smile.

I asked, "Are you ready to test it out?"

Tanner nodded while grabbing his bag. I grabbed mine and opened the front door. There were only a couple of zombies moping around, but not in the way we were going.

While walking, I noticed the zombies weren't decaying like in movies. They looked pale with wild eyes. Anytime they would move it would be erratic and spontaneous. Some of them had blood on their bodies, mostly around their mouth or hands. I would keep second guessing if it's a zombie or not.

After around 5 minutes of walking, I see a zombie in the middle of the road. It was in our way so we knew we had to kill it. It was about 20 feet away and facing away from us. I unsheathed my axes and held them tight in my hands, ready to use them. I had to get its attention, so I brought my foot up and stomped on the ground. It was just loud enough that the zombie heard it and looked in my direction.

It started to sprint at me fast. When it was almost on top of me, I readied my axes but suddenly. Tanner ran at the zombie and swung the katana like a baseball bat aiming at its head. The katana made it halfway through the zombie's brain, making it die instantly. The zombie fell onto its back. Oozing blood onto the concrete.

Tanner cringed, "This is the grossest shit I've ever done." He held the katana with both hands, trying to pull it out of the zombie's head. He stuck his left foot on the zombie's jaw. He pulled up. I heard a crunch before Tanner finally pulled out the katana.

Tanner said with a sigh, "Let's go."

I looked at the zombie's dead body. Its head was split open like a water melon and his jaw was detached from his body. While I was busy looking at the most gnarly thing I've seen in my life. I realized blood from the zombie was touching my shoes. I took a large step back and jogged to catch up with Tanner.

I said. "Yo, I didn't think you would-"

Tanner put a hand on my chest, "shut up."

I was about to go off on him, but he grabbed my shirt and crouched down, bringing me with him. I noticed we were at the edge of a fence and Tanner was sticking his head out, looking at something past it. Of course I had to see what was on the other side. So I stuck my head out above Tanners and my jaw dropped. There were eight zombies in the middle of the road!

I said to Tanner excitedly, "We have to kill them."

"No we don't!?" Tanner whispered, "we can just go another way."

I explained, "The other quickest way will add 20 minutes, and even then, there might be zombies along the way."

Tanner sighed, "Ok, fine let's just do it your way."

I stand up and "quietly" whistle so I can attract the closest zombie to me, but I guess I whistled too loud because the closest three zombies looked in my direction. *So much for taking them one at a time.* All three were sprinters and were coming in fast. Once one of them got close enough, I drove my ax through its head. Tanner ran out from the fence, held out his katana in front of me and the second zombie ran right into it. Splitting the zombies head halfway.

The third zombie was focused on Tanner and he just held his blade in front of him expecting the zombie to run straight through it, but then it moved out of the way to the left of Tanner. He didn't react fast enough.

The zombie pinned him to the fence with a loud BANG. Tanner dropped his katana. The zombie was flailing its arms. Tanner held the zombie's neck with his left hand, and with his right, he held its forehead. It still thrashed around and battered Tanner's arms.

I ran up to the zombie that pinned Tanner, I brought back my right hand and punched the zombie's head. The zombie's head cocked to the left and it fell to the ground. While it was disoriented, I walked over with my ax and stabbed it into the middle of its neck. The zombie started to gag and then pour blood from its mouth.

I took back my ax and walked over to Tanner, "Are you ok!? Did it bite you?"

Before Tanner could speak, the other five zombies saw us and were heading our way. Tanner just barely in time picked up his katana and sliced one zombie's head off. I stabbed another. Only a few zombies were still on the road. Tanner starts to fight one of the zombies to my left. One was charging my way and right before it reached me, I moved to the left and I stuck out my foot. The zombie tripped over and landed flat on his face.

I let out a little chuckle. Then before the zombie could get back up I came up from behind the zombie and sliced my ax through its head. I heard Tanner's sheath and looked at him, he was breathing heavily with both of his hands on his hips. I saw a new dead zombie laid down next to him. I gave him a slight nod and turned to the last zombie.

It was a walking zombie. About 10 ft away. I started to step close so I could kill it but all of the sudden. The walker's head jolted towards me and it fell.

The walker plopped down at my feet and I saw an arrow in the back of its skull. I looked up and saw a full grown man, with a crossbow up to his eye. He had a dog right next to him barking. We made eye contact and he then lowered his crossbow.

He looks at me for a second, like he's trying to confirm something. Then both him and his dog start running at me! He's gonna kill me! I take out my other ax so I have both out. I got ready to fight but suddenly he spoke.

"Miguel! It's me!"

*I recognize that voice, it's him!?*

"Matt!" I yelled back as I sheath my axes.

Tanner said something but it was drowned out by my surprise. I ran to Matt. He then picked me up and hugged me. Crushing my ribs. *How did he find me?*

Matt's my oldest brother, he has long blond curly hair, blue eyes, and a beard. He wears glasses with orange tinted lenses. For clothes, he wore a red hat and blue jeans paired with a brown leather jacket. He's 12 years older than me so he's 28 years old. He moved out of the house and he lives far away so I was surprised he was even here. Matt has a golden retriever. The dog is an old retired military dog so it can do some complicated commands, but retired means that he's really fat, and his name is Simba.

Matt set me back on the ground but still hugged me, "I've been looking for you Mig!" While he was saying that Simba started to rub his face against my hand. Matt let go of me and looked at Tanner.

I turn to Matt, "how are you here? You live so far away."

Matt Took a deep breath, "Before the virus hit I wanted to check up on the fam. Then when I finally reached this town, the crazies started to kill everybody. I ran into a couple's house and thankfully they let me stay. When everything died down I tried to look for Alex, but... he wasn't home. Then I went looking for you, and your house was a mess and you weren't there either. So I've just been surviving now. I'm just happy that you're alive bud."

I turned to Tanner for a brief moment, "By the way, this is my brother Matt." I turned back, "We're going to a friend's house to see if he's there. Wanna come with?"

Matt said, "Of course I will Mig."

Me and Matt walked side by side but strangely Tanner was walking a bit behind us. I looked back and he had a puzzled look on his face. Tanner sped up a little bit to walk next to me.

He whispered, “Is this the other brother I've heard about? I've only met your other brother Alex.”

“Yeah, he's my oldest brother Matt, he lives far away.”

Tanner tilts his head, “Your brother? Why is he blonde with blue eyes and you're... you know, the opposite?”

Matt laughed like a witch, "I'm the black sheep of the family. I'm adopted.” Matt switches the conversation, “Who is this person we're going to anyways?”

I said, “we're looking for an old friend from school. His name is Greg. Do you remember him?”

Matt shook his head, “Probably not, I don't really remember any of your friends.”

“He's the one that would spar me a lot in taekwondo, and he has really long hair?”

“I still don't remember that kid.”

“well anyways we're going to his house”.

I start to see his house in the distance. The most notable thing about his house was that he had a big ball that would shoot water from the top of it, but when I saw it, it was on the grass, broken.

We made it to the front of the house. It looked as good as new, the windows weren't shattered but they weren't boarded up either. The door was closed, it looked like nothing had changed since the last time I saw it. The windows were covered by curtains. Probably so no zombie could see inside.

I walked up to the door, raised my hand and knocked. I heard rustling inside the house. I couldn't hold my excitement to see Greg so I opened the door without a second thought. All of the sudden I got tackled by a person that was inside the house.

I'm on the ground with a guy on top of me in less than a second. He started to raise a metal pipe in his hand and tried to slam it onto my face. I blocked it with my left forearm and punched him in the jaw with my right hand. He rolled off of me and I quickly stood back up. It all happened so fast. The man dropped the metal pipe and it clanked across the ground.

I unsheath both of my axes and hold them firmly in my hands. I see that Tanner has his katana pointed at him and Matt has his crossbow pointed at his head. Simba made a low growl.

The guy started to curse and he held his jaw, "You punch in the exact same place every single time Miguel! I still got a bruise."

I immediately knew it was Greg. I pushed Matt's crossbow down so it wasn't pointed at Greg's head. Tanner put his katana in his sheath and grabbed Greg's left arm to help him up, but Greg swatted him away, "My legs still work." He looked at me, "You just punched me in the jaw." I put my axes in my sheaths.

Greg picked himself up, walked inside his house, and sat on the couch, still rubbing his jaw. The walls were bright yellow and the ceiling was white. All the lights were off but it was still lit from the sun coming through the curtains.

Greg asked, "Can you grab my metal pipe and get ice please?"

I look at Tanner, "You pick up the pipe. I'll get the ice."

Without a word Tanner got up and walked outside to get the pipe. I went to Greg's kitchen and opened the freezer. I looked inside and saw a bag of frozen peas with chopped carrots, and frozen hashbrowns. I grabbed all of them and walked back to the couch. I sat next to Greg and handed him the frozen peas and carrots, he put it on his jaw.

After my adrenaline wore out my left forearm felt like it was on fire. So, to make it feel better I put the frozen hashbrown bag on it. I breathed a sigh of relief.

I turned to Greg, "How did you know it was me before you even looked at me?"

Greg said, "I would remember that right punch from anywhere. I lost count on how many times you punched me in the face, especially in the exact same spot on my chin." He looked at me intently like he had a grudge. While he was saying that, Tanner placed his metal pipe on his lap.

Greg is also a good friend from school. I met him 2 years after I met Tanner. He has dirty blonde hair that's normally in a ponytail. Long hair on top and short hair on the sides. He's taller than me and Tanner and wider to put it nicely. He looks fat but under the shirt he's pretty built. Just got an extra layer of armor you could say. We would spar a lot together, that's probably how he recognized my punch. He's about a year younger than me and Tanner, so he's 15.

Matt walked through the front door, "Hey... Greg, right? Do you have something like a bandage?"

Greg, surprised by the question, said, "Yeah, sure there's some cohesive stuff in the bathroom."

I saw Matt enter the bathroom and he came out with the wrap. Then watched him searching the kitchen counters for something else.

I asked, "Now what are you looking for"?

"I'm looking for paper towels". Matt responded.

Greg says "there inside the top right cabinet".

Matt looked in the top right cabinet and sure enough he found em. I was about to ask Matt what he was doing but I just decided to wait and see.

Matt called over, "Hey you, the skinny one, come here".

Tanner walks over to Matt.

"Sit in this chair."

Tanner followed instructions, and Matt said "Take off your jacket and show me your arms. Tanner just looked at him with a visible confused look on his face.

"Just do it," Matt said, losing his patience.

Tanner reluctantly took off his jacket and placed it on the floor. Tanner revealed scratches and redness all over his forearms.

"Are you ok"!? I ask Tanner in a worried tone. "Will you turn into a zombie!?"

Tanner looked back at Matt with a horrified look on his face but Matt just said, "You won't turn into a zombie, it's only scratches. I got scratched by a lot of zombies and I never became one of them."

I asked, "but it's only been two days since the zombie came in. So it might happen later."

Matt squinted at me, "Miguel shut up for a second."

I see Tanner relaxed his face and he calmed down. Matt put alcohol on one of the paper towels he got and started to clean the blood that was dried on Tanner's forearms. Then after it was all clean he placed new paper towels on his arms and wrapped them with Coban wrap so they would stay.

Matt said, "change them from time to time or when they just get bloody".

Tanner looks at him and says, "How many times have you done this?"

Matt just simply says, "Enough."

After Matt helped Tanner out, I looked back at Greg and asked him, "How is your house in such good condition? Don't the zombies bang on your house?"

"All you have to do is stay quiet, and if they do start banging on your house. Just get out and kill them."

I thought to myself, *if only it was that simple.* It's starting to get dark so I turn on the light in the living room.

I asked Greg "Where can we all sleep?"

Greg said, stoned faced. "I don't remember saying you could stay here."

My heart dropped. Tanner, Matt and I gave each other surprised looks.

The silence between us was broken by Greg's maniacal laugh. "I'm joking, you guys can take my mine and my dads rooms."

I took a massive sigh of relief. After that we all stood around in the living room and started talking about everything. We talked about weird zombies we've seen. What our teachers are doing right now. We talked about everything. After a couple of hours it was well past dark outside. We turned on the light.

I asked, "Can I check out the rooms?"

"Sure," Greg said.

I walked over to Greg's dads room. I twisted the knob and slowly opened the door. I looked inside and it kinda reminds me of a hotel room. His bed is nicely made, it smells dusty, and kind of empty except for the bed. It takes up 80% of the space. I backed up and closed the door.

Right across from Greg's dad's room is Greg's room. So I turned around and opened the door. The first thing I notice is the blast of BO. I immediately covered my nose with my shirt and slammed the door shut with a loud bang. I walked back out into the living room and everyone was looking at me.

"I call sleeping in Greg's dads room." I say still covering my nose.

All the sudden I hear slight banging on the front of the house.

"Got it," Greg exclaimed.

I cut in, "No worries, it's my fault the zombie's banging."

Matt said, "I will help you kill it, just to be safe,"

"No, I'm fine. I can deal with it myself".

"I know you can deal with it yourself, I just want to be safe".

I say redundantly, "Fine, you can come, but just watch".

I unsheath one of my axes and I head towards the front door. I unlock and twist open the door. I'm hit in the face with a chill breeze. It's pretty dark out and I'm now glad that Matt is watching me, making sure nothing goes wrong. I walked out and I left the door open, letting Matt follow. I cut the corner and sure enough I see a zombie banging on the front of the house. The zombie seemed to be too focused on getting into the house to pay any attention to me.

So I slowly walked towards the zombie, making sure I didn't make any subtle movements, and as soon as I got close enough. I slowly brought my ax up and slammed it in its head. It fell onto the grass and I pulled out my ax. I looked back at Matt. He just turned around and headed back inside. The door clicked close. As soon as Matt left I felt like something was watching me. The back of my head started to feel hot and tingly like something was about to grab it. I turned my head violently worried there was a zombie, but there was nothing.

Not nothing, there was something.

On top of a house.

Across the street.

It was facing me on top of a roof.

It looked like a silhouette of a man.

But no man's eyes glow.

They were glowing deep red.

I could see the outline of a man's body so clearly.

I stopped frozen in my tracks trying to study this... thing. It was standing so calm. It didn't even care that I was looking at it. *Was it a zombie? No, it would have started running or walking in my direction. Was it a person? Maybe, but why would they be on top of a house? It doesn't look like they had a gun. It had a black jacket on with jeans I think. It's hard to tell. The whole front part of their body was covered by darkness. All I can see is the outline of their body... and the* ***red*** *glowing eyes.*

My heart was thumping against my chest so loud and fast I thought it would explode. It didn't even have a weapon. I stared at it for an uncomfortable amount of time. It **felt** like I was staring at it for an hour. I **felt** like if I stopped looking at it it would come after **me**.

All of a sudden I heard footsteps to my left. I turned my head. Matt was standing at the corner of the house, looking at me.

Matt calmly said, "Hey, is everything alright?"

I pointed at the thing and said frantically, "There's a thing watching me on the-." I turned my head to look at it but it was gone. I put my hand down. "Roof"

"Which roof?" Matt said.

I turned back to Matt, "It was just there!"

Matt hushed me, "Be quiet, you don't want to attract any more zombies."

I hurriedly grabbed Matt and brought the both of us inside Greg's house. I pushed Matt inside and closed the door behind us.

"Matt, I swear I saw something on top of a roof."

Greg asked, "What's on the roof"?

"Not our roof but the house across the street!" I said fast and nervously. My heart was still pounding violently.

Greg says, "Okay, so what was on the roof?"

I explained anxiously, "It was a man, I think?"

"Does he have a weapon?" Greg asked.

"Didn't look like it." I said, still trying to recall what just happened.

Tanner pulled the curtains to look outside.

I said to Tanner, "He's not there anymore, he left."

"Was it a zombie?" Greg asked like he was interrogating me.

"Give me a second!"

I put my hands behind my head and just focused on breathing. After a moment, I finally relaxed a bit and I continued, "It was staring at me, so if it was a zombie, it would have chased me... and why would a zombie be on a rooftop anyways?"

Greg said, "Soooo it's a person?"

"Maybe, but why would a person be on top of a roof? Also, its eyes glowed a deep red. It was freaky."

Confused, Tanner said, "Its eyes glowed red? Glows how?"

Greg scratched his head, "That's what I was thinking. Like, how would that work? Would it work like a glow stick? Also, since his eyes glow red, does all he see is red from the glow?"

Tanner added, "Maybe night vision goggles-?"

I interrupted them, "GUYS! You're missing the point. The fact is that a random person or thing knows where we live! Aren't you guys even a little worried!?"

Matt said in a calm voice, "Hey, Miguel's right. We should take this more seriously.

"Thank you!" I exclaimed, thankful that someone is actually taking this seriously.

"We should probably stay up late in case it comes back."

By the look on Greg's and Tanner's face, I could tell that they were taking it more seriously after Matt said this. All of us were silent thinking about the situation we were in. I looked over Greg's shoulder to look at the clock and it said 9:32pm. I felt myself calming down more.

Greg said, finally breaking the silence, "Are you guys hungry? I got some food. In the fridge."

I immediately said "Yes."

Then Tanner followed up, "Sure I could eat."

After about ten minutes, Greg cooked up an amazing meal with Matt's help. It was spaghetti and meatballs with a Caesar salad and a basket of cheesy garlic bread. Looking at the food reminded me of the cheese tortilla me and Tanner had this morning.

When Greg Tanner and I would have sleepovers, Greg would always try to teach Tanner how to make food, though Tanner never cared to learn. That's probably why he's a lousy cook. In contrast, Greg is an amazing cook. Since every time we all hang out, he would normally cook the food.

We all sat down at the table and Greg sat out plates of food for all of us. As soon as we got it, all of us except for Greg started to wolf it down.

Greg smiled, "Hungry much?"

I noticed while we were eating, Matt had his eyes on the door, but I was too busy eating to really care about it. I would say Greg is a good cook, but when it comes to spaghetti, he's amazing at it. Me, Tanner, and Greg took cooking classes while we were in high school and sometimes we would hang out and just cook for fun, but man I wish I had Greg's skill to make an amazing bowl of spaghetti. While I was halfway finished with my food, I noticed Matt had a stern expression on his face.

I asked him, "What's on your mind?"

Matt put his fork down and scooted his chair a little bit closer to me. He said, keeping his voice low, "I'm thinking about what you told us about the man on the roof. If what you're saying is true, we're gonna have to leave this house in the morning."

After Matt said this, I got a lump in my throat. I looked over at Tanner and Greg and they seemed deep in the conversation they were having.

I looked back at Matt with a worried voice, "Why should we leave in the morning?"

"The man or thing that was watching you, now knows where we live, and if the man's in a group, then a lot of things can go wrong for us."

"But why would we have to leave? Just because they know where we live doesn't mean we have to leave, right? It's the start of the zombie apocalypse, it is not like they raid us for food."

Matt exclaimed, "You would be surprised what people will do".

This made me confused, "What do you mean? Why else would people raid us? It's not like we have special equipment or anything."

"People at the start of the apocalypse don't raid people for supplies. That's just the bonus. People just do it for the kicks. They do it for **Fun.**"

"How do you know?"

"You should ask the couple I stayed with in this town, or the person that tried to rob me on my way here." Matt paused to laugh, "He quoted a walking dead line too."

I asked concerned, "What happened to the guy that robbed you?"

Matt said bluntly, "I beat the shit out of him, that's what happened, but the point is that we need to move out in the morning. I don't want to risk the lives of you or your friends."

"C'mon Matt, But-"

Matt cut me off and said with a stern tone, “No buts, I’m the adult in the situation, you guys will just have to trust me on this.”

I stayed silent and looked back at Tanner and Greg talking to each other. It felt wrong going into somebody's house and telling them we have to leave it all behind. I get where Matt's coming from, but it still feels wrong.

I'm just hoping I'm right, that the person has no intention of bothering us. I leaned back in my chair because I knew this conversation was over. Matt leaned back too and we both took a deep breath.

After about an hour of us all talking, we all agreed that it was time to go to bed. I quickly went into the masters bedroom because I didn’t want to sleep in Greg's room, which stinks. We only had two rooms to choose from and I knew Greg's dad had one of those super expensive king size beds that's super comfortable.

Not long after Matt walked in with Simba right behind him, he put his backpack down and started to undress. He took off his jacket and hat, then kicked off his shoes. He was left with just a tank top, his jeans and black socks.

Matt just plopped down on the bed and passed out. I thought he was crazy for sleeping in jeans, but to each their own I guess. I laid down on the bed and fell fast asleep.

# Chapter 4:
# "Break a Leg"

Date: 9/13/26

I woke up with my eyes sore. I don't even know why I'm awake. I got up and sat on the edge of the bed. It was still dark and I heard the light tapping of rain hitting the roof. Then I heard another noise. Something not natural. It was muffled and I can tell the noise was coming from outside. Fear washed over me and I completely woke up.

I could barely make out the strange sound. It was like people were talking, but I couldn't make out the words. I was able to hear them in the house right next to us. I also heard a low rumble. I started to hold my breath because I could hear the noises getting closer.

*Are they coming here!?*

I grabbed both of my axes off the floor, and left the room. I ran down the hallway, then halfway, I heard the metal doorknob twist open at the front. I stopped frozen in my tracks.

The door creaked open with a roaring engine filling the house. I can't see the front door where I am in the hallway, but I can make out voices.

I heard a woman say, "Shut up. They're here."

I thought that if I talked to them everything would be fine. Looking back on it, that was probably the stupidest thing I could have done. I walked as quietly as I could to the end of the hallway, but as soon as I reached the end. I stepped on the wrong floor board. making a loud and slow "Crrrreeaak." I held my breath hoping they didn't hear me, but before I knew it, something crashed onto my nose.

As soon as I got hit, my world went blank. Looking at stars on the ceiling. My legs tried to keep me up but I eventually fell on my back. My vision went blurry and my nose felt like it was on fire. I didn't have any time to think.

While I was on the ground, someone's hand grabbed the collar of my jacket and dragged me across the floor. I gripped his arm with both my hands and started yelling for Matt.

I opened my eyes, and I saw a man dragging me to the front of the house. I tried to stand up, but he violently tugged my jacket back to the ground. Then he punched me in the face. He continued to take me outside. I felt the sprinkle of rain hitting my face.

The front of Greg's house was barely lit by the street light. The man let go of my collar in the middle of the driveway. I slowly flipped my body to my stomach. I looked around. The man dragging me, was standing there just looking down at me. I looked over to a truck on the street. I saw that there's a guy inside and another man leaning against the door on the passenger's side.

The man that dragged me said, "Eyes up."

I faced him then immediately got hit in the face. I fell back down and covered my head. I heard multiple footsteps walk towards me. Then something hit my chest, my back, and then my legs. *What should I do? Why? They're kicking me while I'm on the ground.* Two guys continued kicking my legs, arms, and my back. Then, one guy kicked me in the middle of the chest so hard that I threw up.

Everything hurt. I couldn't even think about moving. Then the two guys picked me up by my arms and brought me to the back side of the truck. They opened the tailgate door and threw me inside. I was too weak to do anything. I felt too weak to even yell for help.

The floor of the truck bed was really hard and bumpy. It was so uncomfortable, but I was too tired to care, too beat up to care, too scared to care. All of a sudden I heard a big bang come from Greg's house and then yelling followed. It was a female scream. Then the screaming stopped, abruptly, moments after.

I heard the guys slam the tailgate closed and rushed into Greg's house. I tried to get up, but as soon as I tried to lift up my foot I felt a sharp, stinging pain shoot up my leg. I let out a groan and set my leg back down on the truck.

I was hopeless, I couldn't do anything. I started to feel my consciousness fade in and out. Then, I felt myself starting to pass out.

While I started to feel myself drift away, I heard the tailgate open. I heard a lot of swearing and struggling... It's Greg. I heard two thumps. Then a loud whack followed. The swearing and yelling stopped. After that, I heard rope rustling. Then the tailgate slammed closed.

Greg's voice called out, "Miguel? Are you ok?"

"Yeah" I groaned.

I opened my eyes and I could barely see anything, but I saw a silhouette of a person in the corner of the truck, looking at me. I assumed it was Greg, but in the other corner I saw another person.

I couldn't tell if it was Matt or Tanner. I closed my eyes again and the truck roared then started moving, and it was moving fast. Especially fast for it being pitch black out and raining. The street lights disappeared after driving. The whole ride was about 3 min long but it felt like forever. We finally stopped. A person got out of the passenger seat of the truck and came behind the truck.

They opened the tailgate violently and that made me open my eyes. Greg got grabbed by his shirt. He struggled but eventually got dragged out. Then I watched Tanner get out without struggling.

After he was out I felt someone grab my leg and pull. I felt like I should grab onto something and try to fight him, but I was too weak too. He dragged me by my leg and I dropped on the ground. My head hit the ground first but at least it wasn't hard. I noticed I hit the grass.

"Is he dead?" one guy said.

He let go of my leg. I tried to push off the ground to stand up. I lifted my back off the ground.

"No, He's not." The man pulled my shoulder to face him.

I looked up at him, his hair was long and unkept, he had acne across his face and a dirty patchy beard. He seemed older than me by a couple years. "Just hang on a lil longer. "

At that point I just let it happen. There was nothing I could do. He started to drag me by the collar of my jacket... again. I didn't even fight him this time. He brought me in front of the truck.

While he was dragging me I opened my eyes, all I saw were trees. We were in an open space in a forest by the looks of it. The man let go of me and I just sat there. I looked to my left and I saw Tanner sitting on the end, looking down at the ground. In the middle of us is Greg looking at me. From the light of the truck , I could see him. The side of his face is pink. Probably got punched in the face.

I wonder what my face looked like. Definitely gonna have a bruise in the morning. When I thought about it, I noticed that my forehead was wet, and it felt hot. I could feel it roll down my face. It was too thick to be sweat. Then it fell on my nose. I looked at it.

It was **red**.

Blood. I'm bleeding. From my head. I would wipe it away and more blood would drip. I never bleed this much in my life. I finally snap out of it and look around. I look back to my friends

Tanners sitting down on his legs looking at his hands, with his hair hanging over his face. I looked down and his hands were covered in red. It stopped all the way to the middle of his forearms. *Did he reopen his wounds? Did they hurt him?*

I look forward and I see a blond guy standing in front of us. He has a buzz cut. He's wearing a black tank top with gray pants, and he's just looking at Tanner. His eyebrows twitch, and his mouth points down. He has his arms crossed. Looking at him intensely.

He has Tanner's katana in his arms. It's sheathed and the handle is covered in blood. The guy that beat me up and dragged me is searching inside the truck for something. I looked to the left and there were 2 other guys just standing around. There are 4 guys in total.

"Why are we here?" I said weakly

Blondy slowly turned his head towards me, "Who said you could talk!? I was gonna let you guys off with just a warning, but things change." He turns his head and burns his eyes into Tanner.

"Now I feel like killing some of you"

Tanner said quietly, "I didn't mean to."

Blondy leaned over, "What was that? You have to speak up."

Tanner said louder, with his voice quacking, "I didn't mean to!"

Blondy grabbed Tanner by the hair, "It doesn't matter WHAT you meant!"

He pushed Tanner head down and let go. Then the guy spit on Tanner's face.

The blond guy kept talking to Tanner but I turned my head forward and noticed the man that beat me up and dragged me. Got out of the truck. He walked towards me with something in his hands. It was two axes. MY two axes! He walked over to me and squatted right in front of me.

"These yours?" he said in a calm voice. "You dropped them when you got pounded in the face with that shovel".

He held up one of the axs and made the blade touch my neck. He gently rubbed the blade down. Then he used a little bit more force. I felt my neck needing to itch. He brought the ax back to his body and stood up.

I rubbed my neck. I bring my hand close to my face and I see a smear of blood. Not much blood. He just nicked me. It didn't hurt but it just pissed me off if anything. He threatened me with my own weapon. After all the shit he's done to me. It brought my blood to a boil.

Then out of nowhere I hear leaves rustling, and everyone turns their head in that direction. It's far in front of us. Then suddenly a crossbow bolt shoots out from the bushes and hits one guy in the calf. The guy screams in pain and falls down. I look to my left and I see Greg swiftly lifting up his left leg jean. On the side of his calf I see something shine.

It's his metal pipe.

Greg grabs the pipe and starts sprinting towards the blond guy. Blondy turns around but it's too late. Greg full force smacks the blond guy's left shin. His shin pops and bends the other way. He immediately falls over and howls in pain. One guy runs up and tries to fight Greg with a knife. I look in front of me and I see the guy that beat me up is walking over to Greg with both my axes.

I stood up trying to fight through the pain. I started to walk. With every step I felt like I was about to collapse. Every time my foot touched the ground. I felt an intense pain shoot up my leg, but it didn't matter.

I'm not gonna let my friend die because I'm hurting or tired. He would do the same.

My walking turned into a sprint. I kept getting closer and closer to the man with my axes. He looked to his left and made eye contact with me, but by then, there was nothing he could do to stop me.

Using the last bit of strength I had left. I tackled him and shoved him to the ground. I got on top of him and started to pound at his face. I wanted to beat him senseless. I used both my hands to hit the sides of his face. Right, left, right, left, right, left, right.

As soon as I got all my anger out I felt weird. *Did I just do that? Did I beat this guy?* I looked down at his face and his sunglasses shattered. The frame of the glasses is resting on the ground to the left of his face. I thought he was knocked out.

He violently coughed, "Gonna kill-"

"Oh shit!"

Without thinking, I brought my right hand over my head and punched him in the right side of the face as hard as I could. His head jolted to the left and he slept like a baby.

*"I thought he was knocked out."* I said under my breath.

I looked up and I saw Greg fighting a guy in a hood. Anytime the guy would swing his knife at Greg, Greg would just simply swing his pipe in front of him. Causing the guy with the knife to back up.

I picked up my axes that were by the guy and stood up. The knife guy noticed me get up. I must have startled him or something because he just frantically threw his knife at Greg, missing him completely.

After the guy realized he didn't have a weapon to fight me and Greg with, he turned around and started running. Greg started to chase the guy, but he was too fast and he slipped away.

Then out of nowhere I see Matt come out of the bushes and side tackle the guy that was running away. Matt slammed him on the ground and turned him over. So the guy lied on his stomach. Matt then grabbed his arms and held it behind the guys back. Me and Greg ran up in front of Matt.

"LET GO OF ME!" he yelled.

Matt grunted, "Nope, stand still."

The guy kept wiggling and squirming so Matt grabbed his head and smushed his face in the mud.The guy lifted his head to spit out some dirt from his mouth.

"What the hell man!?" the guy yelled.

Matt called back, "Well, maybe if you stopped squirming. You wouldn't of ate dirt".

The guy finally calmed down and stopped moving.

I said, "Let him go."

Matt was confused, "What? No, I'm not going to let him run away; he still got shit to tell us."

I scoffed, "I didn't mean let him run away, just let go of his hands."

Matt got close to the guy's head and said, "You try to run, I'll shoot you in the leg".

That said, Matt released the guy's hands. He turned his body to face us. He had gray pants on and a black hoodie over his head. The first thing he did was wipe all the dirt off his face. I finally got a good look at him. He was a friend from my school. His name was Bently. He would sit with me, Greg, Tanner and a few other people during lunch. I didn't know him too well but I would still call him a friend.

Greg questioned, "Bentley, what are you doing here?"

"Greg, Miguel!?" Bently said in disbelief.

Greg went over to help Bently stand up but I put my hand on his chest to stop him.

Greg said confused, "He's our friend, let me help him up?"

"I need to ask him some questions." I said sternly.

His voice started to shake, "We can ask them later just help me pick him up."

"**Greg**, listen to me."

Greg just backed up and stared at me. His lip is twitching, and his face is starting to get red. I looked away from him and back at Bentley.

I asked him, "Why did you guys come into Greg's house?"

"I didn't even know it was Greg's house."

I stayed silent and then he blurted out, "I swear!"

I then continued, "Who was that man on the roof?"

His face became confused and said, "what man on the roof?"

"The guy with glowing red eyes that was watching me. Is it one of the guys on the floor right now!"

Bentley's voice shaked, "Miguel, I don't know what you're talking about."

I raised my voice, "No YOU HAVE to know him. How else did you know we lived there?"

I could barely hear Bentely, "No, that's how we found you..."

"Then how did you find us?"

Bently took a long time to think, but then he said, "Me, my brother Anthony, his girlfriend, and a couple of his friends wanted to go to the supermarket to get guns, but when we got close we saw that the front entrance was surrounded by zombies. Then not a moment later two guys start running with a zombie horde right behind them. Some of the zombies broke off from the herd and started to chase us. So we ran. One of my brother's friends wasn't fast enough and died..."

Bently looked down at the ground. "My brother didn't like that. When we went scouting the next day, I saw you and another person walk into Greg's neighborhood. We thought it was the same 2 guys that were at the supermarket. So we waited till night and we searched every house in the neighborhood until... we found you two."

We all stood there processing what we heard.

Bently then blurted out, "I'm sorry I didn't really think it was you and Tanner!"

I shouted, "The man on the roof had to be with you guys he had too!"

Matt shot me a glare to drop it. After he looked at me, I felt stupid for trying to get answers for something that I might have just imagined. Maybe there was no man on the roof, maybe my eyes were playing tricks on me.

I asked my last question, "Why didn't you help me while your friends were beating me up."

Bently stayed **quiet**.

I got everything I needed. Bentley wasn't worth my time anymore. He either didn't care or he wanted it to happen. Either way he wasn't a friend anymore.

**Friends**, don't let that happen.

**Friends** don't let friends get beat up.

"I'm done asking questions." I said, turning my head away from Bently. "Leave."

Bentley became desperate, "Miguel please, I'M SORRY. Please let me stay with you guys. Were friends right? You can't just lea-"

Before he could finish his sentence I threw one of my axes right between Bentlys legs.

"Leave"

Greg grabbed my shoulder, but I just shrugged it off.

Bently said in a quaking voice, "Were friends, Please."

Making my voice clear, "After what happened. You're just a stranger."

I flinched forward. Bently crawled backwards and then got up frantically and ran. I watched him disappear behind the trees. I looked at Greg and tears were just rolling down his face. Not making a sound, I turn my head to Matt. He had his head faced away from me. I looked around and I could see sunlight shine through the trees. I turned my face towards the sky and I could feel water run down my cheek.

# Chapter 5: Anyone Home?

After a bit, I looked back at Greg and he was wiping his tears. My eyes just kept filling up with water, making my vision blurry. I wiped my eyes with my sleeve.

I bent over trying to pick up the damn ax I threw at Bentley's leg. When my hand got close to my ax, my legs suddenly gave out and I fell down. I went to my hands and knees, hovering over my ax. I looked down at it and I started to cry. Vision was so blurry that everything was a blob of color.

I heard someone walk up behind me. I grabbed my ax. Mat quickly lifted my arm and brought me up. Pain shot throughout my whole body because of the jerky movement. I was holding one ax that was hanging in front of Matt's chest and the other ax was by my side. When early morning came, the sun had a yellow shine through the trees.

Matt asked in a soft voice, "What did they do to you?"

I didn't respond.

Greg shouted at Tanner, "Come on. We're leaving."

Tanner stood up and walked over to Blondy who was on the floor. He was passed out from the pain, the shock, or maybe something else. Tanner bent over and forcefully took his katana from the blond guy's arms. He then stood up and spat in the guy's face. While Tanner was looking at him, I could hear him say "Bastard" under his breath.

Tanner started walking towards us with his head down. His white shirt was splattered with blood. His hair was over his eyes and his expression was completely blank.

I looked at everyone on the floor and the only one awake was the guy that got shot in the calf. I watched him trying to pull the bolt out, but every time he touched it he pulled back from the pain. I could feel Matt starting to turn my body in the other direction. I faced my head forward and we started walking away.

...

We finally got to Greg's house. From the forest to the house, not much happened. Matt helped me stand. Greg and Tanner killed any zombies that were in our way. The whole time we were walking, I felt like I was in a daze. I was practically sleep walking. We walked inside and Matt laid me face down on the couch in the living room. Matt placed a pillow under my head and I passed out.

Update 9/13/26:

I opened my eyes. It felt like I just blinked. I woke up extremely groggy and all my muscles were sore. I kicked my legs off the couch and stood up. I started to get light headed. It felt like I was about to pass out. I put my hands on the floor and sat down in front of the couch. With my legs close to my chest and my arms resting on my knees. All of a sudden, memories from the night before started flooding in. Me getting beat up, getting shoved in the back of the truck, fighting, Bentley. I felt so much that night, but now...

I just feel *numb.*

When I think about Bentley now I just... don't feel anything. It's hard to explain. It's like everything I felt that night just isn't there. It's not like I'm ok with everything that happened, I'm not. It just feels like it was a dream, or a nightmare, but the sad thing is I know it's not a dream. I have the bruises and the scabs to prove it.

After staring at the floor and zoning out, I came to my senses. *I'm so hungry,* I thought. My mind was partially awake but my body felt dead. I turned to my left and I saw Matt sitting on the arm of the couch.

"Sup bud." Matt said with his eyes squinted and his voice groggy.

Matt had his head leaned against the wall while the top part of the couch supported his neck.

"Sup", I returned. "How long have you been there?"

Matt just sorta scoffed and grinned.

I asked, "What happened to Greg and Tanner?"

Matt yawned, "I don't know, Greg's probably in his room."

With that, Matt adjusted his head and he fell asleep. I turned back and headed towards Greg's room. I got to the entrance and the door was already open. I saw Greg in the most awkward sleeping position I've ever seen in my life. Belly up, Arms spread out, one leg up to his chest. After the night we had, I didn't blame him.

I didn't see Tanner in Greg's room so I just closed the door and walked away. I turned around and opened

Greg's dad's room. There's no one inside. All I saw was the blanket on the bed flipped to the other side. I looked down and I saw Simba looking up at me. He had this whining face that looked so adorable.

I let Simba out of the room. He walked down the hallway and plopped onto the couch. Simba lifted his head and laid it on a pillow facing Matt, never looking away. I smiled at the scene. Simba was always attached to Matt like glue.

I walked to the bathroom, hoping for Tanner to be in there. I twisted the knob, opened the door and the lights were off. *Where else could he be?* I remembered that Greg has a backyard with a tall wooden fence. That's the only other place he could be.

I walked to the glass door that led to the backyard. I slid it open. I walked through the doorway and the air was warm even though it was Fall. I could feel the sun baking my skin, and there was a gentle breeze that just cooled you off.

It's been a bit since I've been able to enjoy the weather. Much less anything at all. My mind felt clear. I had all the time in the world. No school, no chores I had to get done, no company I had to work for. Even after everything that's happened with the supermarket and the people that beat me up. I thought it was worth it for freedom like this.

After soaking up the moment, I took a deep breath. I looked to my left and there was nothing but grass and the fence. I looked to my right and my heart dropped. It was Tanner, but I didn't recognize him at first. I didn't notice I was smiling, but I felt it drop when I looked at him.

He was on a foldable chair, his hair hanging over his head, and his legs were straight out and spread. His katana was in front of him no more than ten feet. His shirt had splatters of dark red stains all over it. Tanner kind of scared me.

There was a cinder block right next to him. I walked over and sat on top of it. It felt extremely awkward, but it's not like I could go back inside or anything, leaving him like this. I just sat there and looked at the sky trying to think about what to say. I finally just looked back at Tanner. I noticed he was just looking straight ahead.

I followed his eyes towards a patch of dirt next to the fence with a shovel on top of it. The back side of the shovel was faced towards me. It had a spot of blood in the middle of it. I felt a lump forming in my throat.

I stuttered, "What happened?"

Tanner doesn't answer. He looked like he was in a daze. He just kept staring at that one spot

"Tanner, what happened?!"

"Drop it."

"Tanner, you can tell me."

Tanner turned his whole body towards me violently. He brought his head close to mine and yelled, "JUST DROP IT!!!" He was visibly panting and his arms and face were sweating and his eyes were bright red.

It all makes sense now. Specific memories from last night started to flood back in.

I heard a **woman's** voice

Getting hit on the nose with a **metal object**.

While I was in the truck I heard a **female** voice **scream**.

The blond guy was so pissed.

He would look at Tanner.

The **shovel** over the patch of dirt with **blood** in the middle.

**Tanner with blood all over his shirt and katana**.

It all made sense. There were two people in the house. One person was the guy that dragged me out and the second person was the one that hit me with a shovel. A girl. She never came out...

Instead the shovel was laid over a patch of dirt.

That's why the blond guy was so **mad** at **Tanner**.

"Tanner... did you?"

Before I could finish, Tanner's lip started to twitch and his eyes started to water. Tanner slowly turned back into his seat, hunched over with his hand on his forehead. Taking deep breaths.

I thought if Tanner got it off of his chest he would feel better, but it didn't help at all. I started to pat his back.

Tanner's voice would crack, "I thought it was a zombie, I didn't know."

I said in a calm voice, "Do you wanna talk about it?"

"No... I just wanna forget it ever happened." Tears fell down Tanner's face. Tanner wipes his tears with his sleeve, "I needa... shower."

"Yeah, yeah of course"

I grabbed his shoulder and lifted him up. We both walked inside and headed to the bathroom. I put Tanner in and he shut the door. Not long after, I heard the water running. I looked over to Matt on the couch and he had his eyes open and was looking at me.

Matt asked, "Do you know?"

I said with a sigh, "Yeah, I have an Idea."

I walked over to Greg's room and he was still sleeping, but this time he was sleeping on his stomach. I started to rub my hands together, I wound up my whole arm and, "WHACK". I smacked Greg so hard it echoed throughout the room. Greg immediately started to flop like a fish on his bed. Matt practically jumped off the couch and ran to the entrance of Greg's room, with Simba right behind him.

Matt looked around, "What happened!"

"WOOF" simba bark.

I laughed, "it's fine."

Greg tossed and turned, "why'd you do tttthhhhaaaat" he said while rubbing his bum.

I looked at my hand and it was bright red. Matt started to chuckle, after he figured out nothing was wrong. Greg quickly got out of bed and bolted at me, so I quickly ran out until I reached the living room. I keeped my eye on the hallway waiting for Greg to run out after me, but surprisingly he just shut his door. Matt and Simba walked back into the living room.

I asked, "What happened to Greg?"

"He's just taking a shower." Matt said, patting Simba on the head.

After about 20 minutes, Greg and Tanner came out of the showers. In Greg's house there is a bathroom in the hallway and one in Greg's room.

The only reason Greg had a bathroom in his room was only because he won it in rock paper scissors, against his dad when they first got the house. Greg only has his dad, since his Mom left a long time ago. The only reason Greg's dad wasn't in town was that he was in a different country on a business trip.

Matt asked Greg, "Is it alright if we can use your bathrooms?"

"Yeah sure."

Matt and I started heading to the bathrooms. Matt took Greg's bathroom and I took the one in the hallway. I walked in and closed the door. I looked in the mirror and I looked like crap.

My hair was standing straight up, I had a scab on my cheek, and another on my neck. I took off my shirt and it looked worse. The whole front side of my body was covered in bruises. I turned around and looked at my back, but it wasn't any better.

I took off the rest of my clothes, turned the shower knob, and looked at my leg. I thought about how Greg hit

Blondy on the shin. The way it snapped. Just thinking about it makes my shins hurt.

While I was in the shower, Matt washed my dirty clothes and put them on the bathroom sink. When I was done, I got dressed and walked into the living room.

Matt looked at me, "You know you slept for a whole day straight?"

"What, How?" I was shocked.

"Yeah, you plopped down on the couch at like six in the morning  yesterday and didn't wake up until eight today. I would've thought you died if you didn't move so much in your sleep." Matt said with a smile.

"Well, what did I miss?"

Everyone went silent and Matt's smile quickly faded.

*Stupid question*

*I know what happened, even if I wished I didn't.*

After a long pause, Matt scratched his beard, "Well you missed us eating all the food."

Greg lit up, "Why don't we go to Walmart to get food?"

Tanner and I looked at each other like it was an inside joke.

Tanner explained, "Walmart's closed with a lot of zombies inside now. Plus there is barely any food in there anyways."

Matt cleared his throat, "We don't have to go to a store. We can just search a house."

*Huh,* I don't know why but I never thought about looting another house. It feels like it would be the first thing to think about in the zombie apocalypse scenario.

"But what about the people?" Tanner said, "If there's people, they would most likely shoot us."

Matt added, "That's just something we have to deal with, and they're not gonna shoot us out of the blue. People are stupid, but not that stupid." Matt let it hang in the air before adding, "And also, we can't come back here."

Greg said with a visibly confused face, "Wait, what, why? This is my home? Why would we leave it?"

"The guys that found us a day ago will probably come back for us just like last time." Matt looked at me and Tanner, " You guys pissed them off really bad to the point they tracked you down and almost killed you. I thought you guys would kill them but we let them free. They're gonna come back."

Greg slumped his shoulders and bit his lip.

I announced, "If we're going to leave, we better do it now."

...

After a while of packing our stuff, we met in the living room, "Everyone got their stuff?" I asked.

I was hoping for an answer from somebody but Tanner's eyes were staring at the ground. Greg was shifting uncomfortably, and Matt just looked like Matt. I took that as a "yes" so I headed outside. The sun was directly overhead. I looked around for houses to search and almost every house looked clean. Some houses were boarded up, but not as many as you would think.

This neighborhood was full of the same one story houses, with barely anything unique except for the color. Matt started walking towards the house right across the street from Greg's and everyone followed.

Matt got to the door and straight up opened it. Didn't even knock. I couldn't see much, but I heard a middle aged guy start yelling at Matt.

The guy was balding and his beard was gray. He was wearing a gray beater with jeans. The man walked up to the door.

His breath reeked of alcohol, "Who the hell do you think you are barging into my house. You're..."

The Man went silent with wide eyes looking at us. He then started reaching for something around his waist, but before he could finish, Matt quickly brought up his crossbow and pointed it at his head. The guy's eyes got wider and his mouth opened.

Matt said with no room to debate, "Don't move your hands. We are going to close the door and leave. Didn't mean to cause trouble."

The guy backed up. Matt was holding his crossbow with one hand. With the other hand, he slowly reached for the door handle. As soon as Matt grabbed the handle, he slammed the door shut.

"Run," Matt said calmly.

Without thinking I walked down the porch and started sprinting down the sidewalk. I can hear everyone right behind me.

Greg yelled, "WHY ARE WE RUNNING?!"

From behind us, we heard the door swing open and crash into the wall. Not long after, we heard a gunshot. The bullet hit a metal trash can right next to us and made a loud "Bang" sound and the trash can fell over. After seeing that, I immediately made a right turn down another street.

I'm not just going to wait for the old man to catch up to us, so we kept running. While running, there were a couple of zombies on the road and sidewalk. I pulled out my axes and quickly slashed one away. Matt and I were on the right side of the road and Tanner and Greg were on the left side. There were at least 8 zombies in front of us.

Tanner was right beside me and sliced a zombie on his left and I pushed away a zombie on my right. There was another right in front of me that I was ready to kill, but suddenly an arrow from Matt's crossbow stuck through the zombie, in the middle of the forehead.

I was impressed that Matt could hit a moving object ***while*** running. As I passed the dead zombie, I looked behind me and saw Matt swiftly retrieve the arrow from the zombie's forehead. I looked back in front of me and I made a left turn with everyone following.

...

We reached my neighborhood with no zombies in sight. Everyone stopped running in the middle of a four way street.

Greg said, panting with his hands on his knees, "Why did we stop here?"

I take a deep breath, "We're almost there. We're just a 5 min walk from my house already."

Tanner turned to me, "Why are we going to your house?"

"I still have supplies and stuff at my place, and I don't want to repeat what happened with the old guy."

While we were still catching our breath, Matt reloaded his crossbow.

I looked over, "Matt, you need to teach me how to use a crossbow some time."

We all waited for everyone to catch their breath but we mainly just waited for Greg. Greg is not built for endurance, nor speed but at least he can keep up. When we started walking. I tried to look inside the houses to see if there was anyone. To my surprise most houses had people peering through the windows.

I walked backwards to look at the group, "Did you guys notice that people in houses are watching us?"

When I said that everyone started looking at the houses.

Matt pointed at a red brick house, "Yup, there's one."

I looked and saw that the blinds were pulled back by three fingers. I tried to look inside but all I saw was darkness.

Though as soon as everyone started looking at the house. The person quickly closed the blinds. *That's weird,* I thought to myself. Then I looked at all the other houses and most of them were like that too.

*Why was everyone watching us?*

I haven't seen any zombies on my street so far. Probably because me and Tanner killed most of them, but even then there were 2 zombies in front of us. Matt shot one and Tanner sliced the other.

Not long after we made a left turn and I could see my house. Though it looked different. It looked smaller. After taking a closer look. It only took me a second to realize that my house had collapsed.

My heart dropped. I started sprinting full speed towards my house. I stopped running when I got to the driveway. I couldn't believe it. My house was demolished right in front of me.. Pictures, Weapons, books, EVERYTHING... **Gone**.

The house looked like it was cut in two. The house was leaning to the left and there was a car right where the door should be. The car was a truck and it had a cardboard slab duck taped on the back that said, **"THATZ FOR THE LEG"** In sharpy.

*How is this possible?* Those pricks shouldn't have recovered that quickly. Hell Greg broke one guy's shin. They shouldn't even be moving! How? Why?

I heard the guys run right up behind me.

"Shit" Greg blurted out.

Tanner said, "Wait what happened."

"Read the sign..." I said, trying not to yell at him.

I walked over to the street, trying to think about what I just saw. I sat down on the curb with a tree hanging over my head. I put my hands over my mouth and blankly stare at the ground trying to think about everything.

*There's no way they recovered so quickly. So they would have had to have done it when they were injured. Now why would they go through all this trouble when they're injured? Do they hate us that much? I mean, Greg did break the blond guy's shin and I beat the crap out of the guy that beat me up. Though after what they did to us it feels like we should be even.*

Matt sat down to the left of me, "You ok bud? I'm sorry about the house."

I looked to my left at Matt, "Nah dont worry I don't care about the house, I was just shocked at first. I just wish I had my Machete and other things."

I went back to thinking.

*They had to have done it in the last 2 days max. With their injuries I bet they couldn't have gone too far, and since they hate us so much, why would they? There's also no reason to go too far away from my house. Their like us... they just have fun. Even if we have different definitions of fun.*

I stood up and looked at all the houses. I looked towards one, they closed their blinds. I looked towards another. They close their blinds. I looked at all the houses in a row and **every, single, one, closed** their blinds after I looked at them. My heart dropped. Those men could be in any of those houses, watching, planning, anything. I put my hand on the ground and pushed myself up.

Urgently I said, "Matt, we need to leave."

"Leave where?"

"Anywhere but here."

# Chapter 6: Looking Sharp

I turned to Matt, “The guys from the other day are watching us.”

Matt held his crossbow tight, “How do you know?”

“I don't, but they have no reason to be anywhere else.”

I walked over to Greg and Tanner looking at the house, “Guys, let's go.”

I turn back to the road we just came from.

Greg sped up to me, “Are we going back to my house?”

“Like we said before, we can't go back.”

Tanner asked, “Then where are we going?”

“I don't know, but anywhere but here.”

...

After about 5 minutes of walking we made it back to the 4 way road again. It was a quiet walk. My palms were moist in my pocket and my body was steaming. On the way my eyes wandered towards the houses expecting to see those guys.

I looked to the right and I could see a total of 3 zombies until the road slanted down where I couldn't see anymore. I turned to the left and it's a straight path and I only saw one zombie along the road really far away.

I wiped my hands on my jacket, "Lets go left"

"Where are we going?" Tanner asked.

"I have no idea." I turned my head to face everyone. "Where do you guys want to go?"

Matt said bluntly, "anywhere that has food. I'm starving."

"Yeah same" Tanner nodded.

Greg thought for a moment then said, "Ok yeah we want food but what's the main goal?"

Matt turned, "What do you mean?"

"I mean, do we need weapons, clothes, that sort of stuff? What's the goal?"

After Greg said clothes I looked over at Tanner's jacket and It's covered in scratch holes from the zombie that pinned him against the fence. Also his jacket had a couple of blood stains on sleeves that Matt couldn't wash out.

I looked at Greg and he had a pair of jeans and a brown hoodie. His clothes don't look too damaged, but speaking of weapons. Greg only has a METAL PIPE! *I was wondering why his sink wouldn't work*?

Matt said, "I think our goal is to survive. I think that's our main goal." Then Matt laughs. "And that starts with food."

I see Greg's eyes light up, "We should go to the mall! It has everything we need! Weapons, clothes, food, everything!"

Matt scratches his beard, "It's been a while since I've been in town but isn't the mall a 15 minute drive. That's all the way across town, and we don't even have a car."

I spoke up, "What else are we going to do? We aren't in a rush, we can do ANYTHING we want. It's not like we have jobs or need somewhere to be. Let's do what we want!"

After a second Matt said, " Well... I guess you got a point."

I said, "Sounds like we're going to the mall right?"

Matt sighed sure and Greg got a massive smile on his face, "Thank you, It's been a while since I've been there."

Matt turned his crossbow to the front of his body and took aim. I looked in front of me and it's the zombie I saw earlier. Matt shot it between the eyes and we moved on.

...

After five minutes of silent walking, Greg asked, "Why aren't there many zombies? Shouldn't there be a lot?

I scratched my head, "Yeah you're right. It doesn't feel like much of a zombie apocalypse if you ask me."

"Let's hope it stays that way." Tanner said.

Matt joked, "By this rate you guys might go back to school in the next couple of months."

*Just thinking about school makes me cringe. I don't even want to think about doing homework or an essay again, and after everything we've been through? It would be so weird to have a normal day of school again...What am I thinking? We won't ever have school again... right? At least not while I'm around... hopefully.*

Greg seemed kinda happy hearing that while me and Tanner were dreading the thought.

I said to Matt, "Never bring up school or I might punch you."

Greg then said, "School is not that bad."

"Of course YOU like school, you have a crush on our math teacher."

Tanner turned to Matt, "It's true."

"NO NO NO IT'S NOT TRUE!" Greg exclaims.

While Greg was trying to convince me that he didn't have a crush on our math teacher. I could hear Matt and Tanner Burst out laughing. Greg tried to explain himself but I couldn't hear over our laughter.

After everyone settled down, we made a right and It's about a straight path until we made it to the mall. I looked back at Greg to my left and he's looking slightly down with his cheeks as red as a cherry. A zombie wasn't too far away and thankfully it was faced the other way, and again Matt shot the zombie with his crossbow.

...

Not much happened while we were walking all the way to the mall. We had to of passed by at least 30 zombies on the way. The zombies were either trying to get into other buildings, didn't see or care about us, or if they did we would just kill them. Most were walkers anyway. Matt pointed his finger, "Is that the mall?"

We all shot our heads up to look around and sure enough, it was the mall. The Mall had a tan color with a visible glass dome in the middle. The mall is pretty dang big. Around 100 stores. We were on the other side of the parking lot so we were still a bit away. I didn't see any zombies in the parking lot or anything.

Before the zombie virus hit, they closed down the mall maybe a week before the zombies flooded into our town. Same with almost every other store. How people got most supplies was by the stores shipping the products to you, but most people like me just got a crap ton of stuff before the lockdown started. Plus the stores that sold their products by shipping, overpriced the crap of every item. And your boy ain't got that type of money.

Anyways we walked to the back entrance of the mall. The doors were motion activated sliding doors and unsurprisingly they were shut off. The door was made out of glass. We could kinda see inside but it was a little dark.

Greg got real close to the sliding door, looked up and started waving his arms at the sensor.

Matt patted Greg's shoulder, "Step back." Greg stopped flailing his arms and backed up.

Matt brought up his foot and kicked the glass right next to the door and... It didn't break. He didn't stop tho. He kept kicking. He did it 5 or 7 times before he backed up and told us "How about you guys give it a shot."

Greg said confidently, backing up, "I'm gonna throw my Metal pipe at it!"

Tanner cautioned, "I don't think you should do that."

Greg, without listening, backed up 10 ft and turned around getting into position. The rest of us hurriedly walked away while Greg did his thing. I shielded myself with my arms expecting the metal pipe to bounce off and come in my direction. Greg brought the pipe behind his back, took a few steps forward and threw it as hard as he could.

It started to spin in the air and hit the glass directly. The glass shattered completely. Not long after we could hear the very loud and long echoes of Greg's pipe clanking on the ground inside the mall.

Tanner said surprised, "Damn, I thought the pipe would bounce back and hit me."

I chuckled, "I know right!?"

Hopefully there's no zombies inside, because if there are, they will definitely know where we are.

Matt is the first one to get close to the broken door. He kicked the edges of the doorframe that still had remaining glass pieces. When it was clear he crouched down and walked in.

"Are there zombies?" I asked

Matt's voice echos, "I don't see any. Come on."

Greg walked in, then Tanner and I followed. The first thing I noticed when I walked in was that the mall had a crazy eerie feel to it now that it's closed down. I never thought about what the mall would be like when it's empty. It's so unreal. I wonder if I will ever see a mall full of people again...

hope not.

THIS IS GREAT!!! We have the whole mall to ourselves and everythings FREE!! So many things to do! Get clothes! Get weapons, play games, eat, have fun!

Screw buying things! We can just grab our things and go! I was so excited I couldn't help but smile.

After we were away from the broken glass, I brought my arm up and wrapped it around Tanner's neck.

I said cheerfully, "What do you want to do first!"

"Eat," Tanner said.

"Ok fair enough. Oh, I bet we can find some amazing food around here!"

I saw Greg bend over to pick up his pipe. I let go of Tanner and turned to look at Matt. He's walking in front of us looking around. I looked back in front of me.

Just now, we walked in through the back of the mall. The main entrance was on the other side. We were basically in a big open food court. In the center of the room, it was filled with tables and chairs, and on the walls there were a lot of food stores. Normally, you could easily see what stores were around you, but the lights were not on, so you couldn't really tell what anything was. There's a main area of the mall where a massive glass dome is overhead with escalators and a water fountain in the middle. It's located in the center of the mall.

I looked back at Greg and I fast walked to catch up with him. I slugged him on the shoulder. "Why did you want to come here of all places?"

Greg shrugged, "Mainly for the food."

"What's the other reason? I know you got one!"

Greg said with a sly face, "Well I was hoping to swim in the fountain in the middle of the mall."

I grinned "Smartest guy I know. Let's do it right after we eat!"

Right next to us I could see a 7/11 sign. "Hey, how about we eat there?"

Tanner said, "Ok" and Greg followed up, "Sounds good."

I heard a loud creaking followed by grunting. I turned around and I saw Matt picking up a long rectangle table and walking over to the broken glass wall.

Matt calls out, "Can you guys bring two chairs!"

Me and Greg rushed to a random table and we each picked up a chair. As me and Greg were walking to Matt we watched him place down the table in front of the broken glass wall. The table almost covers the massive hole just being a little short on the sides.

Me and Greg set them right in front of him. Matt just placed the two chairs against the table.

Greg awkwardly said, "Uh Matt, we found a general store where we can eat. Is that ok sir"

Matt laughed, "Yeah, of course that's ok. You don't have to call me sir bud."

Greg scratched the back of his neck, "Alright."

We all walked back to the general store where Tanner is waiting.

Tanner said, "I don't think we can get into the general store. The metal gate is blocking the way. I'm pretty sure we have to go somewhere else."

After Tanner said that I looked around and I noticed every store had Metal gates blocking the way. I didn't notice it because it was pretty dark and I was too focused on that we were in a closed mall to pay attention to anything else. I was really bummed when I thought we would have to go somewhere else to get food, but funny enough, Greg walked over to the gate, grabbed it, lifted it up, and it actually opened.

Matt chuckled, "Welp, there you go."

"No way." I exclaimed

Then there's Greg that has a face that found gold.

It was almost pitch black in there and looked like a horror movie, but nonetheless we all walked in there.

After a second, the lights turned on and Greg jumped. We all turned and saw Tanner next to the light switch.

Now that everything was bright, it didn't feel like a horror movie anymore. It's just like a normal general store but it felt like a dream. Every shelf was stocked with everything; gum, candy, chips, you name it! Well... anything you can name in 7-Eleven.

After looking around for a little bit, I realized there's not really any real food in a general store. It's more like snacks than a meal. Even so, I wasn't complaining. We literally had a whole store to ourselves and could eat whatever we wanted.

The 7-Eleven had 5 aisles and the store had the classic green and white theme. On the left wall was the cashier's place, and on the right and back wall were the refrigerated drinks.

I walked over to the right to the drink aisle. I opened the door and got hit with a chilled breeze. The drinks were still cold! I looked around trying to see if they had my favorite drink, and sure enough they did. I grabbed a cold bottle of Nestle's strawberry milk.

You can never go wrong with strawberry milk. If you say Strawberry milk is Mid im ok with that, but if you

EVER say strawberry milk is bad, you're not human, or you just never had it.

Anyways, I grabbed my strawberry milk and I also grabbed a Dr. Pepper for Tanner. I didn't immediately spot him so I went aisle to aisle trying to find him, and of course I found him at the last aisle crouched over looking at chips. I handed him the Dr. Pepper bottle and he thanked me. I walked over to Greg who was stuffing his Hoodie with any food he could find. When I saw him, the only way to describe him was a bloated penguin. His whole upper body looked rugged and sharp. Kinda like a crumpled up piece of paper.

I asked Greg, "What are you doing?"

"I'm getting us food," he replied.

"Yeah... I see that. How exactly are you storing all that food?"

"In my jacket."

...

I'm not even gonna ask how he's doing that. I walked over to Matt and he had a packet of beef jerky in his hand. He was sitting down leaning against the wall with Simba's head in his lap.

Matt looked at me, "Want some?"

"Sure," I reached down into the bag and took two pieces.

I started chewing. After I finished, he handed me another beef jerky packet that was in his pocket. I took it and ate.

After 3 minutes of finishing the packet, I said to Matt, "Thanks for saving us."

"Saving you how?" Matt said, confused.

"When you shot that guy in the calf when we were... in trouble."

Matt shrugged, "Oh yeah."

"We might've died if you weren't there, and it's weird to think about."

Matt looked me straight in the face with a stern expression, "Miguel. You and your friends won't ever die. As long as I'm here with you, I'm never gonna let that happen." Matt then stood up and ruffled my hair, "But that doesn't mean be a dumbass and act invincible. "

I chuckled, pushing his hand away, "Yeah yeah I got it."

After everyone got something to eat, Greg asked if we could check out the stores around us. Everyone was fine with the idea so we started to walk around. It was dark out so it made it really hard to make out the signs on the walls. Then all of the sudden, the mall was filled with light. I looked around confused by what turned on the light and I saw Tanner by the light switch.

Tanner called out, "Guys turn on the light switches! They're right out in the open!"

I stopped and looked around. The mall looked beautiful. I hate being cheesy, but the mall had a different feel knowing that I could have everything with my friends. No more money problems. Just us.

I looked back at a sign that was now glowing blue text that said "Bijoux". Don't know how you say it or what it meant, but me, Greg, and Tanner tried to figure it out for an embarrassing amount of time.

We only stopped because Matt was opening the metal gate to the "Bijoux" store. The metal gate flew up and we all walked in. Tanner turned on the lights. Everything was sparkling. It's a jewelry store! I want everything, but I guess wearing a diamond ring isn't exactly manly. So I just looked around. Jewelry is pretty much dead weight anyways.

Matt was looking around and Tanner and Greg were looking at the chains, facing away from me. I see Greg pick up something.

I walked up behind them, "Whatch you guys doing?"

They turned around and Greg had a chain in his hand. It was a shiny silver chain. It didn't have anything on it. I would think Greg would grab a big golden chain or sum, but he picked a small one compared to other chains I saw.

Greg showed me, "You think it's cool Miguel?"

"Yeah it's cool... but why is it so small."

"Big things come in small packages." Greg said with a grin.

I laughed, then pointed at the other chains, "Sure bro, but wouldn't you want one of those big chains?"

Greg pauses for a second to think. "Not really, My dad had a chain like this... I just want to be reminded of him."

After Greg said that, I thought of my dad. Suddenly my chest felt heavy. The way Greg talked about his dad. I can tell he really missed him. I wish I could have felt like that with my dad... how long has it been since I've seen him? **Too** *long...*

All of a sudden I heard Tanner say something to me but I didn't hear the words. I snapped out of it.

Tanner looked at me, "Miguel you ok?"

I felt a lump go up my throat.

I said smiling, "Dude of course I'm fine... Hey Greg let me help put the chain on you."

Greg handed me the chain and turned around.

*Why do I feel like crying? Don't cry. This is not the place to cry. I can't cry. So stupid, I should be used to it.* I try to occupy my brain with something else, anything else. I'm in the zombie apocalypse, I'm the happiest guy in the world with so much to do! Right?

Greg turned his head, "Are you gonna put on the chain?"

*"Oh right!"* I moved Greg's pony tail and wrapped the chain around his neck. I then snapped it together and pulled his hair back down. After that, Greg started to look around again in the store. I wondered what he wanted now? He started looking at diamond rings.

I asked, "Greg, what are you looking for now?"

Greg smiled, "A ring for my future wife."

I chuckled, "Aren't you thinking too far ahead... got someone in mind?"

"Not anyone really but... this is the best time to get one. If I can get a big diamond ring for free, why not, right?" Greg said with a weird grin.

I didn't know Greg was a ladies man, but you learn something new every day. After Greg found the ring for his future wife, we all left.

When the zombie apocalypse hit. We got 3 days of class before the Lockdown started. Since it was so early in the school year. The back to school supplies were still selling in every store. Including the mall.

While we were walking down the hallways of the mall. In the middle, we saw a cart with back to school supplies. I looked at the cart and got curious. I went over to check it out. It had journals, tape, mechanical pencils and just normal school supplies.

Greg tapped my shoulder, "I have an idea." I turned my head to look at him. He points at the cart, "You should write a book about all our experiences in a journal so we can remember all the cool things we did!"

I liked that idea!

Tanner jumped into the conversation, "And I bet you could draw pictures to make it better."

I didn't like that idea.

"Bruh, have you seen my drawings?"

Tanner looked at me smiling, "What, can't do it?

...

I couldn't tell if he was challenging me or if that was an actual question. Either way, I liked the book idea so I picked up a black journal and some mechanical pencils and put them in my backpack.

I suggested, "Tanner, your clothes are ripped up. So how about we all go to a clothing store and get stuff."

We all agreed and just started to follow Matt with Simba by his side. We walked quite a distance with the occasional turning on the lights. The mall was amazing with the lights on with no other people around except your friends. To get to the clothing shop, we had to go through the middle of the mall with the massive dome overhead. Sunlight was shining down from the top making the floor bright. Then around the center were the escalators that go up to the second floor.

Only one problem, I scanned the ground and there was a person lying on his stomach surrounded by a pool of blood coming from his head. The person had black pants with a blue shirt on. Splinters of glass shards littered around him, and weirdly enough, there was a backpack completely open no more than 10 feet from him with supplies scattered around.

Greg walked closer, "What do you think happened to him?"

I looked up and saw one part of the glass dome was broken, "See that. I think he fell somehow."

Tanner looked at the ceiling, "Are there zombies on the roof?

"I don't know. But... I don't think this guy was a zombie." I replied.

I looked back at the man, and for some reason, he had dirty shoe prints on his back. Also, there were bloody footprints walking away from the body. I had a bad feeling but I didn't know what it was about. There wasn't anything we could do, so we just moved on.

After a bit of walking, we finally made it to the clothing shop. I could understand why Greg and Tanner were getting new clothes, but me? I was practically unscathed, or I should say my clothes were practically unscathed.

The only damage I took during the apocalypse was the beating of a lifetime. My body still ached from them kicking and punching. I didn't tear my clothes. Tanner's blue jacket was covered with scratches by a zombie that pinned him against a fence and Greg's brown jacket was covered in cuts from Bently when he was swinging at Greg with a knife.

Nothing was really damaged, but if I could get free clothes, I'm gonna. I just needed a new jacket for the weather and also protection from zombies scratching and biting me. So I just walked into the clothing store and went to the jacket area. After a bit of searching. I found a cool jacket. It was black, puffy, and had a soft hood with writing on the sides and chest. The writing was in cursive so I didn't even know what it said.

I figured I might as well get other things as well. I ended up taking a gray shirt and a pair of red running shoes. Not gonna lie, I looked at myself in the mirror and I was looking sharp.

After I was done checking myself out, I sat down against the wall next to the entrance of the store, waiting for everyone else to get ready. I put my backpack in front of me, took out my journal, and a mechanical pencil. That is when I started writing our story.

Update: 9/3/27

It sure was taking the guys a long time to get their clothes. I pushed myself up off the ground and started to head in the direction where they should be. After a minute, I found Tanner and Greg walking around.

I shouted, "Hey guys, did you get your clothes?"

They both turned around. Tanner got a dark orange puffy jacket with black jeans. Greg has a dark green hoodie with cargo pants.

I walked up to them, "Nice clothes, do you guys know where Matt is?"

Greg patted his jacket, "Thanks, and last time we saw Matt he said he was taking Simba to go to the bathroom."

I asked, "You guys wanna come and get him real quick?"

I have no idea where in the mall Matt would let Simba pee. So I searched around the area. I started to walk out into the hallway with Greg and Tanner right behind me. As soon as I stepped outside the store, I spotted something out of the corner of my eye. I held out my hand to signal Greg to stop, but he walked past me anyway.

I looked over to my left and I saw a man. I thought it was Matt at first, but he had a hoodie on over his head. He was facing away from us looking down. When I knew it wasn't matt. I thought it was a zombie, but it felt so familiar? I took one step towards it and it shot his head up. After just a second, he turned his head to me and his eyes were glowing red.

# Chapter 7: The Man on the Roof

I whispered to Greg, while keeping my eyes on the thing, "It's the Man on the roof."

Greg said in my ear, oblivious, "Cool?"

I unsheathed my ax by undoing the velcro. It made an echo throughout the hall. The red guy still looking at us, brought his left leg back and his right leg to the front. The Man brought up his arms and started sprinting in our direction.

I heard Greg yell then he ran back into the store. My mind and body screamed at me to move. I immediately turned around and started running back into the clothing store with my ax in hand.

Tanner was a couple steps back in the store oblivious to what just happened, so I yelled, "MOVE IT'S COMING!"

Almost immediately Tanner, Greg and I split up, which is good, BUT IT'S NOT GOOD WHEN THE RED GUY DECIDES TO CHASE YOU! I could hear him running behind me. I had to make several quick turns so he wouldn't be able to catch me.

He's faster than all the other sprinters I've met, and he was coordinated as well. Everytime I took a turn, he would either slow down and turn or push off the wall and turn. Normally with a running zombie they always go max speed, so when you turn, it will take them a while to do so or they would just faceplant into the wall. *This guy was smart and fast. He's going to catch me soon if I don't fight back.*

I ran out into the mall hallway and yelled "Help, I'm over here!"

I turned around and held my ax out head level with my left arm, hoping the red guy would run into my ax.

Nope.

He went to the side of my arm and hit my forearm with brutal force. My arm shot to the right making me lose my ax. I watched helplessly as my ax glided across the floor. I immediately turned my head back and Red was already at my stomach taking me to the floor.

Red was a little bit shorter than me. He had a hood over his head and a black mask covering his mouth. His shoes and the bottom of his legs were covered in blood. I couldn't really see anything else because the only light coming in was from a small skylight overhead.

The man brought up his left hand to attack me. Right before he could strike my face, I moved my head and his hand hit the floor hard. I grabbed his arm. I pushed and rolled. I slammed him on his back and it made a loud thump sound that echoed throughout the place. He lost his breath, then shut his eyes. He quickly opened his eyes and brought his legs up to my chest. He violently kicked me right in the chest. I got sent backwards, stumbled, and fell on my butt. I looked up and he was standing there, watching me with his red eyes.

I frantically stood up and got into my fighting stance. I put my right leg behind me and my left leg in front. I also have my left hand in front of my face and my right hand close to my chest.

Red studied me up and down then copied my hand placement. He walked over to me and threw a left punch.

I dodged his first punch by backing up. He went for another and I deflected it with my right arm. He was a surprisingly slow puncher for being so fast on his feet. By how he's fighting, it's like he's never punched before and his other movements were unpredictable and unnecessary.

After deflecting his punch, I brought up my left hand and punched him square on the chin. It hurt my hand to go bone to bone, but it hurt him a lot worse. His head cocked back and he stumbled backwards. After that hit I wasn't afraid anymore. I knew I could take him. Even having the shit rocked out of him, he still snapped his neck back to me like he wanted more.

I yelled, "What do you want!?"

In return, all I got was silence. *If he wants to play this game, then fine, I'll play.* He walked towards me and started to throw a punch. He threw a left hook and I backed out of the way. He then stepped up and leaned into a right punch. I stepped to the side, and while his right arm was extended I grabbed it with my right hand, pulled him in, and punched him in the ribs as hard as I could.

I felt something crack, and it wasn't me. Not a moment later, he turned and punched me in the face. It hurt like hell. His punching speed suddenly increased and he also followed through with his punch. *I wondered how he was still moving after that blow? He should've been down or at least lose his breath.*

*I don't even know if this guy is human. I don't know which one would be better. Him to be human or zombie.*

I took the blow and backed up a couple feet. It felt like my brain bounced around in my head and everything I saw was spinning. After I regained my balance, I snapped out of it. He hit me in the chin like I did to him. While we were just standing there in a fighting position, I could see Greg and Tanner behind the red guy. They just came out of the clothing store so they were about 20ft away.

I watched them out of the corner of my eye and they had the goofiest way of trying to sneak up. They were hunched over and took tiny little steps. I paid so much attention to Tanner and Greg that I didn't pay attention to the red guy.

The red guy started running at me, pulling back his right hand. When he's practically on top of me, I stepped to the left hand side and kicked his stomach with my shin.

His body folded over my leg. I tapped my foot on the ground and then quickly side kicked him again aiming for his head. I planted my kick right on his nose. He stepped back, but this time I could tell it hurt. The red guy put his hand over his face.

I saw Tanner had his katana out and Greg had his metal pipe. Tanner was about 5 ft behind the red guy. He was crouched and had his katana held out straight in front of him. I knew what Tanner was thinking.

I stepped up to the Red and kicked his chest as hard as I could. He stumbled backwards and fell right on top of Tanner's katana. The katana slid right through the left side of his stomach. Red's mouth opened and he let out a horrible scream while gripping the blade.

The scream was high pitched and extremely loud. The echoing was making it so loud I had to cover my ears. I started to feel light headed. The scream lasted what felt like forever before it abruptly stopped.

Red stood up and the katana slid out of his side. Red took a couple of big steps away from us then turned around to face us. I could have probably beat him myself, but with Tanner and Greg, it's absolute. *What do we do with him after? I didn't want to kill people, but is he even a person?* I heard something that sounded like car keys shaking. I looked to my right and I saw Simba and Matt running towards us.

Matt shouted, "YOU GUYS ALRIGHT!?"

I shouted back, "YEAH, BUT THIS RED EYED DICK IS TRYING TO KILL US!"

Matt just turned a corner but was still a bit away. I turned my head towards Red. He started to hunch over as he put his right leg behind him. Red then put his head down and his hands up, getting into a sprinters stance.

Tanner just STABBED the guy and he acted like it didn't even hurt! I don't know what type of zombie this is, but it's definitely not human. I kind of find that reassuring. Like I'm just killing another zombie, not a person. Then I had an idea.

Red started sprinting in our direction. He jumped and launched himself at Greg. Greg grabbed Red by the shirt. He then twisted his body behind him and threw Red on the floor. It then rolled and landed on its stomach. It immediately picked itself back up and came after us. Greg put his hands up ready to swing.

Red brought up its right arm and punched Greg square on the chin. Greg's body turned to the left and I could hear him cursing to himself. He had his right hand on his mouth, his body facing away from Red.

Red probably thought it was a perfect time to hit Greg in the back, but I knew it wouldn't work. Greg always played dirty when he was pissed. Red was just running, about to hit Greg but He pivoted his foot, swung his upper body, and backfisted Red on the side of his face. Red's chin cracked to the side and he stumbled over himself.

After that, I think Greg and I viewed it as a competition. More of a game without saying it, ***who could kick Reds ass the most.***

I walked over and uppercut Red's stomach and then pushed him over to Greg. Red looked up and immediately Greg punched him right in the ribs. I gave Red a right hook to the face and he stumbled over.

Greg tried a right hook of his own, but Red blocked his punch and scratched Greg on the side of his face. I saw blood dripping from Greg's cheek. I stepped up and grabbed Red by his jacket. He wrapped his hands around my wrists and headbutted me. It was like my mind went blank. I couldn't think of anything. My whole world started spinning and my eyes filled with water.

I started blinking rapidly, holding my head. I wiped my eyes and saw red in the middle of the mall walkway looking right at us. He was about 20ft away from us. I was about to walk toward him, but I felt something was off. I just couldn't put my finger on it.

I noticed rumbling in my chest, and not long after I could hear faint talking it seemed? It kinda sounds like when the neighbors are having a party but all you can hear is the muffled celebration.

Tanner cuts in, "Hey guys, I think we should leave."

All of a sudden, a WAVE of zombies turned the corner and started frantically sprinting towards us. Zombies filled wall to wall. I ran up to Greg who was in front of me. I quickly grabbed Greg's collar and dragged him with me as fast as I could the other way. Greg's brain finally reached his legs and he started sprinting with me. While running, I saw my ax on the floor and swiftly snatched it off the ground. Tanner and Matt were 10 feet ahead of me as we ran away from red.

*I looked behind me and I saw Red standing in the middle of the hallway, watching us run away. It's like he doesn't care about the swarm heading in our direction. He's just fixated on us. I watched as he disappeared into the swarm, and his glowing red eyes vanished. I still see that image in my head. I don't think I'll ever forget that, and I don't think he will either.*

I looked back in front of me and I almost ran into one of those mini stores in the middle of the mall's walkway. I quickly moved to the right of the store and followed Matt.

I yelled, "WHERE WE GOING!"

Matt yelled back, "DON'T ASK ME, I KNOW SHIT!"

I looked behind me at the horde. I can't even tell how many there were. All I knew is that we're screwed if we don't do something quick.

I got an idea.

I shouted, "FOLLOW ME!"

I started running to the main area with the dome overhead. When we made it to the end of the hallway, we took a left turn down a dark hallway and I could see it in the distance. I looked behind me and the zombies were at MAXXIMUM 100 ft away! I looked back and Tanners was in front of me by a few feet and Greg and Matt were running by my side. We made it to the main area and the whole bottom floor was lit up. Leaving the second floor dark.

I yelled to Tanner, "GO UP THE ESCALATOR"

Tanner went as fast as he could up the escalator with Greg and Matt close behind, and me lagging even further behind. The escalators were taller than I remembered. When we made it halfway up, I looked behind me and the horde made it to the escalator. Right before the last couple of stairs I had to climb to make it to the top. I looked up and I saw Greg. "DUCK!" He yelled.

I immediately dropped and laid down on the ground as close to the elevator stairs as possible. My face was pressed up against the cold metal stairs and I felt something rush past overhead. I lifted my head up and turned back. Only then I saw a rectangular table fly its way down the escalator. It hit the escalator, "BANG!" The table kept tumbling down, wrecking the stairs.

The table made one finally jump at the bottom, directly hitting the zombie horde. I saw blood squirt out from one of the zombies that got hit, but it didn't matter. The zombies crawled over what was left of the table and the rest pushed it over and off the escalator. I couldn't tell if pushing it off was intentional or not.

Greg yelled at me, "Bro move! we gotta go!"

He leaned down and grabbed me by my arms. He got me to the top. We took big steps away from the escalator.

I spoke while keeping my eyes on the escalator, "Greg, Tanner, remember when we were kids we went to the roof of the mall that one time."

Tanner added, "Yeah, the security guard came and kicked us out. Why the hell does it matter!?"

I shouted at Tanner, "Remember where we left!"

Greg exclaimed "The fire escape on the side of the building! But, how'd we get there?"

Tanner cursed while pointing at the wall, "Well maybe if you looked up with your pair of eyes, you'd know where to go."

I looked up where he's pointing and I saw a sign pointing towards the fire escape. When I thought we were good, the zombies got to the top of the escalator and started rushing towards us in packs. I got a jolt of adrenaline and quickly looked at Tanner.

He was running next to the glass railing. I followed right behind him and we were off. Not too much running later we turned left. We entered a food court strip and in the middle I saw the fire escape. I ran ahead of Tanner. When I got close enough, I pushed open the door, turned around, and held it open. Tanner ran in, followed by Matt then Greg.

I tried to close the door but a zombie burst in and pushed me against a wall. It started to batter me with his arms.  I grabbed its forehead with my left hand and I grabbed its shoulder with my right.

When I thought it couldn't get worse, the zombie started opening its mouth and it kept getting wider and longer until its jaw was hanging at its chest. Their mouth was outlined with ugly, blood stained teeth and don't get me started on the morning breath. Right then I thought he was gonna chomp my face off.

Tanner came up from behind and his blade sliced right through the zombie's throat. Tanner then pushed the sword downwards and its body started pulsating blood. Tanner slid his blade out. I pushed the zombie to the left and it fell down the stairs making a blood trail. It stopped halfway down and went limp. I wiped the blood from my hands onto my shirt.

I looked around. We were standing on stairs made of concrete. Greg and Matt were holding the door closed to keep the horde from getting in. The zombies were banging relentlessly and they seemed to be getting stronger by the second. Me and Tanner went up to the next level of stairs.

I shouted, "Let's go!"

Matt gritted his teeth, "DAMN IT!"

Matt and Greg let go and ran up the stairs. Immediately the door flew open and the small stairwell was filled with frantic zombies. So many came in at once that they ran right into the wall and some fell down the stairs.

I turned around and booked it up the stairs. I'm going 4 steps at a time to make it up to the next story. I grabbed the railing to the left with my hand and swung myself to the next set of stairs. I kept going until I reached the top. I saw the door and I rammed into it with everything I had. The door quickly swung open and hit the wall. I ran out and the first thing I saw was the setting sun. It made everything bright orange.

*Can't focus on the sun.*

Looking ahead past Tanner, I saw the stairs for the fire escape. *It's not too far now.* I pushed my legs with all my strength. Tanners was waiting at the start of the stairs. I ran next to him and grabbed onto the metal railing. I looked back and Greg was running towards me. Just passed Greg, I saw Matt exit through the door. He was running frantically while swearing like a sailor. The whole group made it to the stairwell, and we started going down. Matt and Tanner were cursing and I was freaking out.

Then there was Greg making random distressed yelling.

We made it half way down the stairs and then I heard the zombies' screams again. They must've made it through the door. We finally made it to the bottom of the stairs and I felt a wave of relief. Almost like we survived a horde of zombies. As I put my arms up and whispered "victory." A zombie fell all the way from the rooftop onto the concrete right in front of us. We all yelled. Then another body falls next to the other. We then realized, we're not done running yet.

# Chapter 8: Mistakes

Date: 9/13/26:

We ran until we got to a small neighborhood about a mile from the mall. We searched until we found an empty looking house. The house looked abandoned, with no cars in the driveway. The curtains were opened and the grass was well overgrown.

We found that the house was completely empty; no food, no furniture. Basically, there was jack squat. We still searched every room for zombies. Thankfully we didn't find any. We placed our stuff in the living room while Matt closed all the curtains. The living room had nothing but a clean white carpet. With nowhere to sit, Greg and I put our bags on the floor and sat against the wall. Matt sat down in front of us with his legs crossed.

"Im gonna take a shower." Tanner said while putting his backpack next to mine. Tanner then walked away and I heard the bathroom door close behind him.

Greg spoke first, "So, was that the same red eyed guy you saw at my house?

I turned to Greg, "Yeah... I wonder why he was at the mall."

"Do you think it was a coincidence or on purpose?", Greg asked.

I thought about it, "Maybe a coincidence? At least I hope so. It would suck if we had a red eyed demon after us just because I looked at him funny."

I looked at Matt's lap, "Wait, where's Simba?"

Matt turned his eyes to the ground, "When the zombie screamed, Simba went running. I tried to get him, but I couldn't.

"I'm sorry dude." I said putting my hand on Matt's shoulder.

Matt shrugged, "I knew Simba wasn't gonna last long. He's a dog after all. I just wish he didn't run."

Greg leaned in, "Are dogs able to become zombies?" I punched him on the shoulder. For saying that after Simba probably died.

Matt sighed, "Apparently, I've seen some zombie dogs while driving here. But for some reason, Zombies never went after Simba."

"ZOMBIE DOGS?!?!" Greg exclaimed, "How dangerous are they?"

Matt answered calmly, "Not too dangerous. It's just a dog, right? I don't know if they can infect you or not, or if there's some type of rules for infecting things, but anyways. What was that thing you were fighting?"

"The red eyed zombie?" I replied.

"Yeah"

I stopped to think about the mall, "I don't know what the red guy really was, I'm pretty sure it was a zombie. But it just wasn't normal. It was smart and copied the things I would do, and learned how to fight back. I think the worst part was that it seemed to not feel pain.

Matt questioned, "You believe that thing will come back?"

"Like I said, I hope not." I smirk, "But it's kinda like we have a roster of villains already."

Matt glared at me with a confused look, "What are you talking about?"

I raised my hands, "Well think about it. The red eyed zombie is like a villain, and the "guys" at Greg's house are like evil side characters."

Matt looked at me with an even more confused look, "You say that like you're happy about it? This isn't some videogame. These are real things that are dangerous."

I shrugged, "I mean... is it not a lil cool to you?"

Matt paused for a second then began to laugh and ruffle my hair, "I mean. I guess you weirdo. I don't understand you sometimes, but you're a teenager so you're gonna be a bit weird."

I pushed his hand away from my hair, "I'm not weird, just optimistic."

Matt laughed and then got serious, "I guess we have to have a talk about weapons now due to the situation. Soon we have to get guns." Matt looked at Greg and I. "But you guys are dumbass teenagers so theirs rules that you need to know." Matt then turned to me, "What's our rules?"

I said for the hundredth time. "1: Keep your finger off the trigger until you're ready to fire. 2: Never face a gun at anybody. 3:Clean your gun regularly."

Matt was the first and only person to ever teach me how to shoot a gun. We went to a gun range and he taught me how to shoot all types of guns. From that, he taught me those 3 rules.

"I'm gonna add one more rule." Matt said with a heavy heart, "Use the gun as a last resort. Things can get messy fast when using a gun, especially with people... and second, just because you have a gun, it doesn't make you invincible. Too many people die from their ego or stupidity."

I said dismissively, "I got it, I'm fine. You don't have to worry."

We heard the bathroom door swing open and slam shut. Tanner  came stomping out with completely dry hair and was wearing the same clothes.

"The water ISN'T running." Tanner said flatly

I stood up, "Wait, really?"

I passed Tanner and walked to the bathroom. I opened the bathroom door and went in. I twisted the faucet and... nothing. I thought maybe it was just the bathroom. I immediately walked into the kitchen and turned on the sink... nothing.

Greg was right behind me, "Wait, is the water out? For how long?"

All of a sudden I hear glass break outside and we all rush to the front. Matt turned off all of the lights in the house. We peeked through the living room window to see what happened.

It was dark out. The only way we could see outside was from the dark orange street lights. We saw a man trying to break into the house directly across from ours. There were broken shards around his feet. He reached through the broken glass and opened the front door. A woman from inside screamed. The man walked in anyway.

The neighboring house door opened and another man came out yelling. *I think he's trying to protect the woman.* Then another person came out, and another. The people coming out would use this distraction to break into other homes or try to protect their neighbors. It became a war zone. It was like when the zombies first entered our town

Everyone was fighting in the street. Ruthless. There were people with all sorts of weapons trying to get in or protect their homes. The streets became littered with people. We were paying so much attention to the fight outside that we weren't focused on our house.

The front door **creaked** open.

**Someone's inside.**

Matt quietly ran behind a wall while we watched. I saw a silhouette of a man walking into the living room. His footsteps were masked by the screaming and yelling outside. Greg, Tanner, and I were hiding in the dark.

As soon as the man stepped one foot in the living room, Matt yelled running and tackled the man. A deafening gunshot erupted throughout the house. The blast lit up the pitch black room. He only shot 3 times before Matt took the gun out of his hand and threw it to the other side of the room. All I could see was a shadow of Matt bringing his fists up, and pounding the man.

The man was struggling, kicking his feet, flailing like a desperate animal. The man's legs slowly went down as the screaming stopped. Matt stopped punching when the man went limp. Matt just stayed there for a second looking, staring. He then stood up, pushing off his knees. He turned towards us.

Matt said with a long pause and out of breath, "He's uhh.... Knocked out. Are you guys ok?"

Suddenly we heard the backdoor open.

A voice erupted from the back of the house, "Hey Tim, are you alright!?"

Matt waved his hand to follow him. We made it to the hallway connecting all the rooms and a voice yelled, "Is that you!?" followed by rustling.

I run to the front door, swing it open and run out. I'm blasted in the face by smoke. There's a house on fire next to us. People are fighting everywhere. I ran out into the street trying to dodge all the fighting going on. At the time, I didn't even know where I was going. I was just running without purpose except surviving. I lost sight of where Tanner, Matt and Greg were. Suddenly I bump into two people fighting.

Without looking, the guy I bumped into turned 180 degrees and swung his bat at me. I ducked and leaned my whole body away from him, tripping over myself. I landed on my butt. The guy that swung his bat faced me, but before he could do anything the guy he was fighting hit him on the back of the head with a club. He immediately collapsed to the ground at my feet. The guy that hit him stared at me. He had the "your next" type look, and I didn't want to see what happened next.

I frantically picked myself up, and ran away. I tried to slip by the crowd to leave. *Easier said than done.* I would pass people left and right. I would take sharp turns or push off of someone if I lost my balance. But then I got careless and ran into somebody.

I started stumbling but I quickly caught myself. I think his elbow hit me in my stomach because he knocked the wind out of me. I was hunched over, holding my body. I about threw up but forced myself to hold it in. I turned around and looked up. He was already facing me.

Before he could hit me I ran up and pushed him to the ground. He stumbled back and fell. I got on top of him and tried to knock him out. He would grip at my face and neck trying to get me off. He then brought back his arm and punched me in the face. I fell off. He then reached for something at his side.

"NOOO" I yelled, reaching for his arm.

I grabbed it and tried to get whatever he was reaching for. I got it from the back of his pants. A gun. *He was gonna pull a gun on me*? He lunged at me trying to get it back. I kicked his face and stood up, pointing it at him. He was trying to plead with me, begging on the ground. But my finger was already on the trigger.

*I shot him. He screamed, and tried to crawl away. I shot again. My ears rang. My chest started to shake. I just kept shooting. Bang... Bang... Bang. Their fighting turned into a panic. Everyone was scared and running from me.*

*I didn't need to kill him... but, I'd be lying to say I didn't want to.*

# Chapter 9: Aftermath

Update: 10/25/26

It's been 42 days since tap water ran out. Also 42 days since that event... Matt heard the gunshots.

He ran over to me, "STOP, STOP STOP!"

While I had my weapon raised, Matt grabbed the gun and took it out of my hand.

"MIGUEL WHAT ARE YOU DOING!"

I've never heard him yell before.

He grabbed my wrist forcefully. "We have to go."

Later, we found Greg and Tanner along the road. We found them on the side of a house with their weapons drawn. They were together. After that, we ran and didn't look back.

Tanner and Greg didn't know what I did. They heard the gunshot but had no idea it was me. When we reached a safe place Matt pulled me aside and we had a long discussion. It ended with him taking away the gun. Which I understand. I never wanted to hurt a human...

The 42 days were pretty difficult. We would go house to house, store to store. It always felt like if we stayed in a place too long. Someone or a group of people would enter. And it did happen, but normally we always out numbered them so we all minded our own business.

Water is not too easy to come by, Senses there's no tap water, we have to find water bottles or something drinkable. It weighs our backpacks down a lot. Which makes travel harder. You don't know how loud water bottles squeezing together makes until you try to sneak past a dozen zombies with em.

Zombies increased in population. All the fighting for water and other things killed a lot of people. Though it didn't happen immediately the streets and houses were littered with bodies. It wasn't until the second day that most of them were running around. Tanner kept tabs. He said they come back as zombies 2-3 days after getting bit. Kinda like the walking dead. Tanner also noted that girls turn into zombies faster than boys. I don't know if he's right or overthinking it but he said it's a thing he noticed.

Runners increased a lot too. Before there was probably a fifty fifty with walkers and runners. Now I can barely find one walker. I noticed runners have a twitchy way of moving. Like they are itching to kill a person. Their heads move fast and every move they make has power. While walkers seem slow and tired. Barely moving their body if not chasing something. They move their heads slowly and mouths hang open. I can't seem to find out why there are walkers and runners and not just one or the other. Though I notice a lot of walkers are skinnier than most of the runners.

Greg got a scar from the fight in the mall. Red must have been sharpening his nails because it left 2 marks, starting from his cheek going down to his chin. Tanner hates it but Greg and I think it looks cool. Plus it's mostly healed now at least. Just a bit red.

Also we found a different zombie type, We call them chompers. One day we walked into a building. More like a factory. I didn't know what they were making there but there were a lot of machines. We were hoping to find somewhere safe to sleep, but first, we had to clear out the place. We opened a heavy door to get in and everything was pitch black.

We brought out our flashlights. I walked over to a metal box and smacked it. It made a loud boom that echoed throughout the building. I heard groaning and yelling from the zombies inside. Thankfully it only sounded like a couple. So we stayed inside to fight.

We were in a square room with tall metal boxes on one side and the rest was open space. Before going to the building, we came up with a plan for fighting in the dark. Two people would stay back and light up the area with their flashlight. The other two would be the ones in the middle of the room fighting.

It was me and Tanner's turn to fight. Greg and Matt went to the corners of the room to light the room from there. Tanner unsheathed his katana and I pulled out my right ax. The groaning got louder until one runner ran through the corridor. Tanner quickly took action.

He stepped to the side then brought his katana back and sliced through one of the zombies' raised arms. When the zombie turned around, Tanner quickly struck its neck with the end of the blade. The zombie fell to the floor. While it was bleeding on the ground, another zombie walked in.

This type of zombie we have never seen before. The zombie emerged out of the dark with its chin to its chest and its mouth wide open. Instead of looking at me and Tanner. The zombie immediately went after Greg who was holding the flashlight. Greg was about to take out his metal pipe but, at the last second, he jumped out of the way. When the chomper ran past Greg, the muscle of its cheeks tightened and its jaw shot up to his head. It crunched and his head popped up. It turned to face us.

Its mouth looked abnormally big. The sides of its mouth were made entirely of muscle. The front of its mouth was littered with teeth.  It tried to open its mouth again, but its sharp teeth were stuck in its lips and gums. Before he could take another step, Matt put down his flashlight and  shot a crossbow-bolt right through the chompers head.

I think the first time I saw one of those chompers was when we were in the mall, but so much was happening, I didn't pay it much thought until one attacked Greg. We've dealt with them a few times after that, but they're pretty rare. Gotta be careful because one chomp and you could probably lose a limb.

# Chapter 10: Bad Things happen

Date: 10/26/26

Matt sighed, "Hopefully there's some water in this building."

I said optimistic, "There has to be, this place is huge."

This building looked two stories tall. It seemed to be some office building too. From the front, you can see through the windows. There were desks, chairs, dividers, the basic stuff.

I laughed, "Greg, remember when you threw your metal bar through the glass door at the mall."

Greg tilted his head, "Do you think I have to do that now?"

Before I could say anymore, Tanner ran up to the doors, grabbed the handle, and pulled it open.

Greg joked, "Awww shoot, I was hoping I could do that again."

Tanner held the door open for us to pass through. I was walking right behind Matt and as soon as we entered the place, it had an overwhelming smell. It was pungent. Something I never smelled before.

I quickly held my nose and searched around. The place was dark and quiet. When Tanner walked in he found the light switch and turned it on. The bottom floor was filled with bright white light. It felt like a school classroom. After the place was lit up, I almost immediately found the source of the smell...

In the corner of the office there was a body. It was rotting. Sitting against the left wall. Must have been there for a while. A couple of days? Weeks? Months? I don't know. The smell was awful, and the body looked worse.

Thankfully I didn't end up like that guy. If I didn't barricade my house, the same thing would have probably happened to me. I wouldn't be with my friends, having fun. I thought in the back of my mind, *I wish he could have enjoyed the apocalypse like us.*

I started walking around scouting out the place to see if there were zombies. I first checked all the offices. Thankfully I didn't find anything. There were no signs of zombies.

The place was a computer office. It was filled with tiny spaces with computers, desks, and other work things. It had 5 foot tall dividers, so you couldn't see each other. There was also an upstairs. It was too dark to see anything. There were stairs in the middle back of the room that split upwards. Under the stairs there were hallways that lead to the back of the building. The downstairs already looked boring so I was more interested in going up.

I shouted across the room, "Hey! I'm gonna check upstairs, you guys check the hallways down here."

Greg followed, "I'll come with."

We got to the stairs and walked up. I made it halfway up and felt like a bat. I reach around and pull my flashlight from my pocket.

*Click*

I could finally see. I looked around but I still couldn't find the light switch.

I said, "Greg, go up the other stairs and see if the light switch is that way."

As Greg walked away, I made it up the stairs and turned right. There was a 3 foot tall rail wall. Walking along a narrow walk path, I took a few steps forward with my flashlight facing the floor. I shined the light up and just a few feet from me, was a zombie. Staring straight at me.

*Shit!*

Before I could turn around or even touch my ax, the zombie launched at me. I tried to punch it in the head, but the punch barely hit the side of its head. It grabbed me by my clothes. I tried to fight back, but he came so fast. It pushed hard and I fell. I hit my head on the wall and fell on my back.

The zombie got on top of me, chomping and screaming. I tried to move its relentless hands. I skimmed his chin and then I kicked him in the chest. It got off and I quickly stood up. As soon as I did, it launched back, pinning me against the wall.

"Miguel!" I heard Matt yell.

I grabbed the zombie by the forehead so it couldn't bite me. I punched with my other hand and tried to kick its legs.

I punched it hard in the jaw and it stumbled back a few steps. While disoriented, I put my hands on its chest and shoved it as hard as I could. It fell head first over the railing. I watched him flip backwards. He went down flailing his arms and then his neck hit one of the dividers. Blood squirted out from his neck and a bone poked out from the back. The zombie immediately went limp. Right at that moment, Matt ran to my side looking over the railing.

We both stared at the scene for a moment.

Matt slowly turned to me, "Are you alright?"

"...im fine"

*I thought I was dead.*

*It all happened so quickly and ended so brutally. I thought the building was safe. I thought I was safe.*

Matt said softly, "Calm down, you're ok."

It sounded like Matt's voice was quiet and muffled.

"Miguel, breathe."

I noticed I was panting. I started taking big deep breaths.

Im alive,

I'm not hurt,

I'm good,

I'm fine.

I started to relax. My breathing went back to normal, but my mind was still racing. *I could have been in school right now. Talking to friends. Complaining about homework. Excited to play video games at the end of the day...*

*Who am I kidding? I've dreamed for the zombie apocalypse to happen for a long time.*

*Right*

*Happiest kid in the world, I got everything I asked for.*

*Right?*

*Got my friends and brother and we have fun everyday in the zombie apocalypse!*

***Right?***

I calmed down, my mind started to calm down, "That was crazy."

It felt like hot sweat was running down my face. I wiped the side of my head. I looked down and saw a little smudge of blood.

I looked at my hand puzzled, "Huh, it doesn't hurt. Does it look bad?"

...

It didn't look bad, but after the adrenaline wore off it burned like hell. Matt found some ice in the break room, put it in a ziplock bag, and gave it to me. I just put it on my face because the zombie smacked me a few times.

**One** zombie. Just **one**.

I got my ass kicked because I was unprepared. In the zombie apocalypse you ALWAYS have to be prepared. **What if he bit me?** Game over, I'm done. No restart. I can't let that happen again. I never want to be that scared again.

We searched the whole building and found a room that was occupied with a couple of walkers. We just kept that door closed. When Greg opened the door you could hear him yell across the entire building. Followed by a slamming door.

"DON'T OPEN THIS DOOR!" Greg warned.

We rushed by to check on him and Greg was fine, but panting. leaning against a door. I pushed him aside and there was a sign of paper taped on the door that said "zombies inside."

I looked at Greg pointing at the paper, "Maybe read next time. I know it's hard for a monkey like you, but still."

Greg kinda just rolled his eyes and walked away.

We then checked the rest of the rooms on that floor and everything was clear. Greg and Matt were doing something on the first floor. Tanner and I were chilling on the stairs leaning against the railing. We just started to talk, "How are you doing?" I asked.

Tanner sighed, "Well I'm not dead soo... pretty good I guess," as he gave me an awkward thumbs up. I looked out the window. It was a dark sunset outside. To avoid attracting any zombies or people. We always leave the lights off and just use our flashlights.

Suddenly, I hear a bang on the front door. Is it a zombie? I looked over the railing. It's hard to make it out but it looked like a person banging on the door. I started to walk towards the stairs but then. ***CRASH***
One of the glass double doors shattered.

I could hardly make out a voice from the door, "Be quiet!"

**People**

Another tired voice said, "We've been out all day, give me a break."

One of their hands poked through, unlocking the door. I watched the hand pull back and not a moment later, the doors opened. One guy walked through, then two, then three! The ceiling lights turned on and off in a flash. I ducked my head and faced my back to the wall railing. *Did they see me?*

A person called out quietly, "The building lights are too bright, search the building with your flashlight."

*They're gonna find us if we don't leave this building.* Tanner was crouched right behind me. I looked back and peeked to the left of the rails. It was a straight path to the front door. With short offices to the left and right. I tapped Tanner on the leg to follow me. I stayed low to the ground and walked the narrow path. Then suddenly, a shadowy figure stepped in front of the door.

Tanner and I scrambled to try and find a hiding spot. I jumped to the right while Tanner ran to the left. I entered an office. As soon as I got through, a light shined down the narrow path. I looked in the office trying to find a place to hide. I pushed out the rolly chair and frantically hid under the desk.

I pulled the chair against me and put my hood over my head. I was wearing all black, so I tried to cover my head and arms in my jacket. I heard footsteps walking fast. Someone was searching through all the offices. I saw a flash of light hit my office and then it disappeared, almost instantly. *Was he even looking through the offices?*

It seemed like his footsteps stopped at the bottom of the stairs. Then I heard the stairs creak.

I pushed the rolly chair as slowly as I could, so it wouldn't make a sound. When the chair was out of my way, I crawled to the exit. I looked towards the stairs and the guy that walked by earlier was going up them. Still looking at the stairs, I crawled to the exit.

Before I could turn around, I saw a light hit the back of my head. I turned around and saw a man blocking the path. All I could see was a bright light. My heart stopped and my eyes went wide.

The man spoke, "What are you doing he-"

Suddenly the guy's shoulder jolts forwards and screams.

Matt Yelled, "RUN! GET OUT!"

Tanner ran out of an office. He passed me and when he got to the guy, he pushed off of him to get to the front door. The guy fell back and hit the office wall hard. He was wheezing on the ground, looking down at himself. There I see a crossbow bolt through his chest. In desperation, he yanked it out. His face was screaming, but all that would come out was gurgling blood. Blood started to pool from his mouth and dripped to the ground.

Matt frantically lifted me up by my arms, "RUN!"

I rushed past Matt and burst out the front door making the glass shatter. I saw Tanner standing in the street looking back at the building. I ran next to him and turned around. Throughout the building there were flashing lights shining throughout the windows.

I saw Matt run to the front door. Before he could get out, a man out of nowhere side-tackled Matt and they both fell down, out of sight. I tried to run to Matt, but Tanner yanked my jacket, unwilling to let go.

"WHAT ARE YOU DOING?! MY BROTHER NEEDS US!"

Greg stepped in front of me. "We can't run in there, There's too many! we have to go!"

"NO!!"

Tanner yanked me back, "Matt said too!"

As I'm getting dragged away by my friends, I watched Matt get back into frame holding a knife over his head. The last thing I saw Matt do was drive a knife through a man.

# Chapter 11:

# "That's a Promise"

Date: 10/28/26

It's been two days since we lost Matt. The worst thing is I don't even know if he's dead. He could have been fighting or just ran away, tortured, or turned into a zombie? Damn it! The zombie apocalypse is supposed to be easy! We should have had walker zombies. People helping each other. Instead, we lost Matt, people trying to kill us, Zombi-

"Miguel," Tanner said softly. "You alright?"

***What do you think?***

I turned my head away, "I'm fine."

I wrote down my final thoughts, then put my journal in my jacket. Since we lost Matt, we ran and survived on food we found along the way, and now we're just sitting in a lobby of a big building. We were supposed to search the building for anything useful.

But I just don't care. I haven't really cared about anything the past couple of days. My mind was still stuck on that night. The night I lost Matt. I was so **stupid.** I should have helped fight off those guys. I should have done anything **BUT** run away!

Tanner tilted his head towards the staircase, basically telling me to follow him up. I couldn't help but follow with my head down. Memories from Matt come flooding towards me.

7 years ago:

I was 9 years old. “Owww” I yelled.

Matt was teaching me how to ride a bike... or, at least trying to.

Matt leaned over me, definitely pissed, “Miguel, If you're gonna crash. Don't hit a car. ”

I looked up at him from the ground. I scraped my knee on the concrete and my right hand was bleeding.

Matt picked me up by my pits. "Come on, you gotta walk it off."

I tried to stand on my hurt leg but pain shot through it. I leaned against the car to minimize the pain. Matt picked up my bike and gave me the handles.

Matt looked at the car, "Dang, you really hit that car hard. There's a dent on the side."

I tensed up, "Wait! Really?" I took my hand off the car to look at it.

Matt started laughing, "No dummy. But you should've seen the look on your face!"

I say annoyed, "Not funny." "Pretty funny," Matt smirked.

Suddenly a house door flies open. "HEY, DID YOU KIDS JUST TOUCH MY CAR!?"

Matt's voice started shaking "H- Hi Neighbor, we were just-"

Before Matt could finish I hopped on my bike and petalled as fast as I could. I heard loud footsteps to my left. "KEEP PEDALING!" It was Matt.
He was running right beside me.

I peddled faster and faster. I turned right, I turned left. I kept pedaling until Matt wheezed, "Stop." I turned around and Matt had his hands on his knees gasping for air. I turned back around on the bike and put my foot down.

Matt said, still wheezing, "I think we lost him."

I asked skeptical, "Are you sure?"

Matt looked up at me, "Mig did you see his gut? I'd be surprised if he can jog."

I laughed.

"And I'm more surprised you can ride a bike. Much less turn." After he said that I realized what I've just done. I exclaimed "I rode a bike!"

Matt added, "And all it took was for someone to yell at you. I should have done that sooner." I was so excited, but then I remembered the car. I said with my head down. "I'm sorry about hitting the car."

I heard Matt's footsteps walking towards me. Matt ruffled my hair and I looked up. Matt said softly, "Don't worry, That guy was a jerk anyways."

Every time I would think about it I'd laugh. Now I feel **sick**.

"Ready?" Tanner said.

We searched the second floor and then went onto the 3rd. It's a regular work building but every floor had something different. Haha, there was this one time.

When I was 12 I asked, "Hey Matt... did you have a girlfriend at my age?"

Matt said, "Yeah of course." like it was obvious

I asked sheepishly, "How do you ask a girl out? Or start talking to them?"

Matt simply said, "Why? Is there a girl you like?"

I looked at the ground, "Well.... Maybe."

He chuckled, "Yeah, I had a girlfriend when I was 12."

It's been a while since that talk and I don't remember much after that. He taught me stuff that no 12 year old should know. That was Matt tho. Unpredictable and uncensored.

Greg caught me chuckling to myself. "What happened? Is something funny?"

I stopped smiling. Remembering that all the good stuff was in the past, and now I'm here... **Sulking.**

We made it to the next floor, and almost immediately, I saw a Taekwondo sign. I remember the only reason I signed up for taekwondo.

I was 13 getting my ass handed to me by my brother.

Matt taunts me to stand back up, “Common let me see what you got!”

“No!” I yelled, “I'm tired of getting my ass beat!”

Matt looked at me disappointed and with a harsh tone, “So? Are you giving up?”

I looked up at him slowly, “...No but”

Matt cut me off and stood over me, “No buts, why would you give up. If you want something you have to fight for it. You wanna get stronger right?”

“Yeah,” I said sheeplessly.

“Then grow some balls and act like it. I can't take care of you all the time. There's gonna be times where it's. Really hard... but you still have to get up, and you're gonna have to do that yourself most of the time.”

I looked at a picture of our parents. I took a deep sigh and got back onto my feet.

He looked me in the eyes, “Good, now throw a punch.” He lifted up his hand.

I brought my fist up and punched, stepping towards Matt. I made contact with the top of his hand.

“Weak” Matt says coldly.

"Well I'm trying!" I yelled abruptly. "If I'm so weak, teach me!"

Matt stood in front of me. "Well, the first thing you gotta do is widen up your stance." He pushed my chest and I stumbled back. "You see? No structure. Have your right foot back and to your right a lil bit."

I did as he said, "Ok, now what?"

"Now put up your hands."

I put both my hands in front of my chest. Clinching tight.

Matt grabbed my left hand. "No no," he lifted it up in front of my chin and away. "I like to keep one of my hands chin level and my other hand close to my chest."

I tried to copy his description completely.

"Good, now you're getting it." He chuckled, "Maybe you're not so hopeless after all."

I say under my breath, "Tsh, shut up."

He said calmly, "Now slowly, throw a punch."

I extended my right hand forward and brought it back to my chest. I looked at Matt waiting for his reaction.

Matt snickered, "Bruh, don't extend your arm."

I gasped, "The hell you mean not to extend my arm! That's the point!!"

Matt tried to quickly quiet me, realizing his mistake, "Shush, I said that wrong. I mean all you do is extend your arm. You don't put your body into it. Let me teach you. First you wanna twist your hips in the direction of where you want to hit. Lift up your left hand."

I had my left fist clenched in front of me.

"Thats what you're aiming for. When you're ready to punch, bring your left arm shooting back and your right arm forward while twisting your hips."

I took a deep breath, my right leg behind me and to the right a bit. Same thing with the left side, but opposite. I brought my right hand to my chest and my left hand in front. All in one motion, I twisted my body and threw a right punch.

I looked back at Matt waiting for approval.

Matt stood there looking at me. "... It was alright."

I turned my whole body towards him. *YEAH RIGHT! IT WAS GOOD, JUST ADMIT IT!"

Matt laughed, "Sure, whatever, it wasn't bad. I'll give you that, but don't let it go to your head!"

"You're a little too late for that." I said smiling to myself.

Not long after that I started taekwondo with Matt's help. He signed me up when I found the dojo I wanted to train at. Later on, Greg started going there and we would go everyday together all the way up until the zombie apocalypse happened. That day, there was a lot of stuff Matt said that didn't make sense at the time... but I'll always be grateful.

When I was fourteen, Matt, his roommate and I went to a shooting range.

I pointed at a gun display case, "Matt, doesn't that revolver look like Rick's revolver?"

Matt studied it, "Yeah it does."

We searched the place and picked a gun we wanted to rent. The walls and floor were dark oak and everything looked clean. After a while, we finally agreed on a Glock 17 to use for our first round of shooting. We bought foam ear buds. We started walking towards the range but then Matt put a hand on my shoulder.

"Remember the two rules?"

I looked up at him. "One, Keep your finger off the trigger until you shoot. Two, when holding any gun, ALWAYS point the barrel towards the ground."

"Good. There's a third rule, but these aren't our guns so don't worry about it. Now that you learned that, let's shoot."

We walked inside. The shooting range was pretty empty. Out of 8 rows, there was only one girl who was shooting a big gun over to the left of us.

We went all the way to the right side of the range and loaded up the glock 17. We hooked up our shooting target. It was a basic blacked out man with a bullseye in the middle of his chest.

Matt clicked some buttons and sent the shooting target out 30 feet. I reloaded my gun, took aim, and fired. Bang.. Bang. Bang.. Bang.... Bang Bang Bang.

After shooting, Matt brought the tarp back still looking brand new. With maybe a bullet hole next to the target dummies head.

Thankfully over the years I got better at shooting. Before I knew it, we made it up to the roof of the building. In front of me was Tanner and Greg looking over the town. Greg took a quick look before declaring he had to take a crap. I didn't look back, but I heard the door open and close.

The sky was clear and there was a subtle breeze. The sun was right overhead. Must've been evening. I walked over to a ledge to look over the town.

There's cars scattered all around. Broken glass was all over the concrete next to buildings. Zombies were roaming looking for their next meal. Even with all this destruction... It was peaceful. I caught my breath and thought about everything with a clear head. I almost forgot about Matt being gone. **Almost.**

I heard footsteps come up from behind me.

Tanner's voice called out, "Miguel, talk to me."

I tilted my head to the right to face Tanner, "What? Talk about what?"

Tanner said with a concerned voice. "You're acting diffrent...your eyes are on the ground, your not joking anymore, what's up?"

I scoffed, already knowing what this was about. "You already know what's up."

Tanner gave a subtle nod, "I do but, I need to know from you."

I felt a sting of anger within my chest, "What's up is that I ran away from my brother in need of help."

Tanner sighed looking at me, "You and I both know he said to run-"

I turned my head and cut him off angrily, "So what!? My brother needed help!"

"And we're safe, because we listened!" Tanner's words were churning my stomach. "There was nothing you could have done... We're not some heroes in a movie. We're just kids."

There was a long pause before I spoke. "But we could have still tried..."

Tanner sighed, "If we tried, we would have ended up the same way as Matt or dead. Your brother helped us and gave us a chance. Plus we don't even know if he's dead or not."

I looked at a broken down car, "He might be out there..."

Tanner started nodding, "And we're not gonna find him sulking around right?"

I smirked at his comment, "Ok ok I get it. I'll lighten up."

Tanner patted my back. Something he never does, "And when we find the people who did that. We will find a way to get back at them and find Matt."

I turned away from Tanner and looked back at our home town with a new Goal.

"I'm gonna find Matt, let's promise."

"I promise Miguel, we will." Tanner assured me.

Suddenly the door to the roof opened. Greg walked over to us and studied our faces, "Huh? What's up with you guys?"

# Chapter 12: Strangers

Date: 10/31/26

Greg called out, “Hey guys, isn't this Hunters neighborhood?”

I looked at the houses, “Oh shoot your right! Hunter Luis, right?

Greg said excitedly, “Yo maybe we will find him.”

We started following Greg to Hunter's house. We killed several zombies on the way. Eventually, we made it and the house was...

“This place is a wreck.” Greg blurted.

The windows were smashed and the front door was wide open. Pieces of the door frame are chipped away. I started to get a familiar sick feeling in my stomach.

I said quietly, "I don't think I wanna go inside.”

Tanner blankly looked at the house, "Yeah, I think that's for the best."

We continued walking down the street. There were little to no zombies along the way. Then, we saw a building in the distance. It's our high school.

The high school is pretty big. It was two stories and had two full sized gyms. So at least that gives you an idea. Our high school is different from what it used to be. Now there's graffiti on the walls, dark red almost black spots on the grass, and one of the wall windows was shattered.

Tanner asked, "Why do people want to break into a high school?"

I said "Why not? How many times have you wanted to run, scream or break stuff in the class?"

"Not much," Tanner said bluntly.

I look at him, "That's probably just because you're boring."

Tanner ignored me and we walked into the high school through one of the broken windows. We took a look around. There was more graffiti inside everywhere saying either #### you or just trashing on the school in general. The place was also dusty, gross looking, and smelled rotten. I saw one dead body that reeked. Must have been here since the start of the apocalypse. There were a bunch of insects festering around the body. Rotting... gross.

We passed the body and entered the lunchroom. The room was empty with tables folded and stacked against the walls. Chilly. Light was shining through the wall of glass.

Greg's voice echoed, "Now what?"

All of a sudden, yelling erupted behind us. As soon as I heard it, I snapped my body towards the noise. The sound was coming from the east side of the building.

"HELP ME!" A faint voice called out.

Without thinking I start running in the direction of the screaming.

Tanner ran behind me, "Miguel! We don't know what's happening!"

I ignore him and keep running. I speed pass the lunch room and make it to the gym entrance. I come to a stop and stand in front of the big metal doors. I try to open them but it feels like it's stuck. I try to push it open but no use.

Greg grabs my shoulder, "Stand back!"

I back up a little bit to the right. Suddenly Greg charged at the door, with his arm shielding his body. The door burst open with a loud BANG. Tanner and I rushed into the gym, following Greg in one clean motion. We stopped to look around to see what's going on.

The Gym is a wreck. There's parts of the ceiling on the floor. Gym equipment scattered around everywhere. Bleachers down. Lights out. The only reason we can see is because of the holes in the ceiling. There was a guy that was screaming. Right in the middle of the gym. He had a hood on and a shadow covered his face. I looked around one more time and it's only him.

I walk over, “Hey, are you ok?”

He brings up his hands and says with a shaky voice, “Woah woah stay back!”

I tried to defuse his panic, "Don't worry, we're here to help. Just tell us what happened-”

“Are you with him!?” The man cut me off.

There was a moment of confused silence before Greg spoke, “With who?”

The man started speed walking towards us, "There's a... a thing here that's been following me the past 3 days.” He says with genuine fear in his voice.

He starts to throw his hands around like he's going crazy. “He goes wherever I go! He's not a zombie but he's far from human, and and he's here! Right now. I don't know where he is but-”

He suddenly stopped talking when he got close to us. I could see his eyes lock onto mine. His aura completely changed. He has a familiar look. He had a patchy beard. Dirty face and clothes. Deep blue eyes.

Oh. My. God.

"Miguel?" His voice echoed in my head.

It's Bently.

His voice changes from fear to anger, "Miguel!?" He grabbed me by my collar. "You left me to die!"

Tanner tries to step up, but I hold my hand up for him to stop, "Bently"

I said, trying not to lose my stomach. "Bently... what happened, how are you-"

He cut me off again, "Alive? I had to fight for myself for the past month! Because of you!!" Tears started rolling down his face and he tugged at my shirt collar, "You told me to get! I had nowhere to go! I never found my brother... I had to find a different group. Then they kicked me out..."

He got quieter and started to trail off on words I couldn't even understand.

I grabbed his hand and pushed it down, "Bently... I.. I"

"I what! TELL ME!" Bently said sharply.

Tanner stept up and pushed Bently's chest away, "Calm down!" Tanner yelled.

Suddenly a door slammed closed. We all turned our heads towards the loud bang, but there's no light in that part of the gym. Only darkness. My heart practically jumped out of my chest.

"It's back..." Bently said, shaking.

Suddenly I saw something in the darkness. Two distinct red eyes stared at us without a body. Flashbacks of the mall come rushing back. The man on the roof is back. The floating eyes started walking towards us, and before we knew it. It was there.

No more than 20ft away. Wearing a hood and a mask. You can still see where Tanner stabbed him. Dark red is smeared across the left side of his jacket, with a gaping hole. His clothes were ripped up and down. Though he looked scarier than he is. We beat him last time so we can do it again. Bently said the red eyed guy just followed him. He's never fought him before. Bently doesn't know how weak it is.

I kept my eyes on Red's body. "Bently don't worry, this guy looks scarier than he is. We beat him before."

"...What?" Bently said, confused.

I said confidently, "If we work together we can beat him. He's just a guy... I think."

I took out my axes from my hip and placed them both in my hands. With that I heard Tanner take out his katana, and Greg took his pipe out of his pants(metal pipe).

Greg looked at Bently and asked, "What do you have?"

Right after Greg finished, I heard sprinting behind me. I turned and saw Bently run full speed towards the gym door. Before anyone could react, a piercing sound shot through the air. I tried to follow the noise, but it's already too late. Suddenly, there was a loud dull thud that hit Bently. He fell on his arm, clutching the back of his leg.

"AAAHHH!"

Before the object hit Bently I got a glimpse of it. It was a knife. I turned back to the red eyed zombie. He draws back his arm from where he threw. He then turns to us. Me, Greg, Tanner.

Red's gaze made my blood turn cold. He has a different feel to him since the mall. And... is he taller? I take a quick glance at Greg and Tanner and they both have the same look.

*Can't focus on that. He was easy last time, right?*

I tell Greg and Tanner while Bently's cry echoes throughout the gym, "Lets kill this thing."

Greg said with a panicked voice backing up, "I'm sorry, but I have to help Bently."

I heard Greg jog away.

With that, Red is tracking Greg with his eyes. I walked towards Red with axes in hand ready to fight. He didn't move an inch, just watched. I took a couple fast steps and swung with my right arm. He moved to the left and kicked my side. I stumbled back. While Red had his back turned watching me, Tanner went behind him and swung his katana like a baseball bat at his head. Red ducked, turned towards Tanner and grabbed his legs. He lifted his body off the ground then let go. Tanner fell on his back. Red looked down at Tanner beneath his feet.

I come towards Red with one of my axes over my head. I put all my body into it and slammed it towards its head. But at the last second Red moved his body to the side and my axe smashed the floor between Tanner's legs.

My ax connected to the floor and rattled my whole body. It made a loud pop and shot itself off the ground. Tanner jolts backward quickly picking himself back up.

After I regained myself. I look up from my ax to Tanner. Before I knew it, Red brought his fist up and slid it across Tanner's face. Tanner fell to the floor.

"NOOOO!" I yelled.

I brought my ax over my head to swing again but red turned around and punched me in the gut.

**I cant breath**

-

**I cant breath**

-

**I cant breath**

I clutched my stomach and turned away. All I could do was wheeze and quick breaths. I tried to shuffle myself away from red. It's like my lungs didn't work anymore. Red grabbed my hair from behind and threw me to the left. I stumbled, facing away. He kicked my knees and I fell, wheezing. I saw Tanner feeling his jaw. I crawled over to him.

I tried to say something. Anything. But all that would come up is wheezing. I grabbed Tanner's jacket. He quickly got to his feet and helped me up. I finally get a gasp of air.

Tanner pulled me away, "Miguel we have to go!"

I said between gasps, "Where's, Greg?"

I scanned the gym and I saw Greg carry Bently to the gym door.

Greg yelled out, "I'm getting Bently out of here!"

I finally caught my breath and yelled back, "We'll cover for you!"

Tanner hit my chest with his arm, "Miguel! we can't beat this thing without Greg!"

I yelled back, "Then what the hell are we supposed to do!?"

"MIGUEL!" Tanner shouted, pushing me. I stumbled back, and in the corner of my eye I saw a flash of black strike the air. I turned my head and red had a long knife pointed to the ground.

*Did Red try to strike my head? Of course he did but, if Tanner didn't push me out of the way I would be* ***dead****. The knife that Red had looked like a bowing knife.*

Bowing knives have a longer blade and a spear-like point at the end, but Red's knife looked dull and the end was chipped off. Although it was chipped off, it still looked sharp, and the silver blade was stained in **dark red**.

Tanner grabbed my shoulder, "Miguel, we have to lose this thing-"

Red swung his knife at Tanner but he dodged. We took a couple steps away. I extended my left ax in front of me and my right ax held close to my chest ready to swing. But before I could attack or even think about running away, Red started sprinting towards the gym door. *Shit he's going after Greg.*

Me and Tanner book it after Red. He burst through the door turning to the left. The door closed before me and Tanner slammed the door open again. We looked to the right and there's no sign of Red, but there were only two ways to go.

Tanner tried to protest, but I already took the left hallway. I kept running, looking around to see any sign of where Red could be. I glanced into the classrooms, looked into the halls, nothing. *Where could he have gone?* Suddenly I heard screaming and yelling come from behind me. Sounded like Bently.

Red didn't turn left when he ran out of the gym. He went **right**.

I start sprinting back to where I came from. The yelling continued until it randomly stopped just down the hall coming from the science classroom.

I burst through the door and my heart sinks to the floor. Red has his back facing me. I took a step inside and looked past Red. There I see Greg.

**I'm too late.**

Greg is laying against the wall with blood splattered across the floor. Greg. ***Now? What? How?***

I can't think. One of my best friends is down.

No, no, no, were supposed to live.

Sadness swept my head and I started to lose my balance. I looked back up and Red had his knife in Bentley's throat. Red threw him to the ground and turned his head to look at me.

That bastard

Zombie

Psycho

Monster

He's sick. I'm gonna kill him, I lowered the axes in my hand so I'm holding the end.

"Im gonna kill you." I said with absolute certainty.

Red's eyes squinted and its mask got wider. Is he smiling? Is this a game!? I charged at him swinging my axes. *Swing swing swing that's all you can do. Bastard killed them.*

He dodged all my strikes. He'd backed up, ducked, partied. I couldn't touch him, but suddenly he grabbed my left arm and pulled it behind my back. I know what he was gonna do before he did it.

While holding my wrist with his left hand. He brought up the other and struck my elbow.

*POP*

"AAAHHHHHH"

I stumbled away looking to the side. My arm was bent at an unnatural angle. It's so bad I started to tear up. I turned back around to Red and suddenly my vision turned dark.

Another flash of pain shoots through my eye and blood squirts out.  A warm wet liquid runs down my left cheek. I bring up my right hand and my eye feels like mush. Red then pushed me.

The force violently sent me to the right. I stumbled and fell. I tried to catch myself on a table, but only my fingers caught it and I slipped, hitting my head on the edge. Immediately as I hit the floor, my wrist made a weird sound. I screamed from pain

I turn over on my back. While I placed my left hand down on the floor. Pain shot through my hand. *Damn it, I need to get out of here.* I bring my attention back to reality. I'm face to face with the devil, and he's towering over me.

No No No. FEAR. I backed up frantically, kicking my feet and pushing off the ground with my right hand. FEAR. My whole head is burning hot. FEAR. I try to look for anything! ANYTHING!! FEAR. Somewhere to run! Something to throw!!

I backed into the wall and it almost made me jump. FEAR. Red stood in front of me and I couldn't move. FEAR. Everything in my body said to, but I couldn't. FEAR. He looked down on me but I can't match his gaze. FEAR. I kept my eyes locked on his legs. FEAR.

Feeling hopeless. More than hopeless. I tried to think, but I couldn't. I tried to calm down, but I couldn't. My breathing quickened. Reds just staring, not making a move. Cant even read its face!

There's movement behind Red's legs. Can't make sense of it until it was already right behind Red. He turned around.

Greg's voice screamed out with his metal pipe over head, "AAAAAHHHHH!!!"

Greg sprinted towards Red and smashed his head in.

***Crack***

Red fell to the ground. The only sound escaping his body is his bones breaking. Greg got on top of him.

Greg bashes again. "HOWS THAT!"

***Crack***, He swings again, "DOES IT FEEL GOOD!"

***Crack***, "ENJOYING THIS!!"

***Crack***, "WAS IT WORTH IT!!!"

***Crack***

***Crack***

***Crack***

***Squish***

# Chapter 13: Howdy Neighbor

I'm backed up against the wall. The only sounds in the classroom were me and Greg's breathing. Bloods splattered all over Greg's chest and face. There's blood dripping off of Greg's pipe, and at the end of the pipe.... shit.

I turned my body to the right and threw up all the food in my stomach and more. After a few minutes of gaging. I turned around. Greg's just staying there, looking at the mess. I look back down and want to throw up, but I can't.

Got nothing left to throw up.

Red's face is... is it even a face anymore? Just a splatter of mush and.... Nevermind, I don't want to think about it.

Greg stood up first, one hand clutching his stomach, and the other gripping his pipe. Blood seeps through his hand. I pushed off the ground.

I asked Greg "What did he do to you?"

Greg looked down at his stomach and back to my face. He opened his mouth like he was about to say something but he stumbled back like he could barely stand up. I rushed over to him and grabbed his arm with the right side of my body.

My voice trembles, "Common Greg stay up."

Panic for my friend shoots up my throat, "HELP! SOMEONE! ANYONE HELP!!"

All I got in response was silence. I turned my head to Greg. His head is down with his eyes looking at the floor.

I said in Greg's ear, "Greg, we need to get out of here."

Greg blinked slowly and moved his head up and down, "ok ok."

With that I carried Greg and walked towards the classroom door. I look to my left and I see it again. Him again.

Bently

Head down with his blood coming from his neck. *If I helped him that day in the forest? Would he have ended up like this? Could I have done something? Did I make the right choice?*

Suddenly Greg groaned, taking me away from the thoughts from my head. Panic washed over me again and I headed towards the door. We shuffled our way out.

My voice echoed throughout the school hall, "HELP! TANNER!!! WERE OVER HERE! GREGS HURT!!

I waited a second to see if anyone would respond.

I yelled again, "HELP! US!!!"

Suddenly I heard loud stomping and yelling, "WERE COMING!"

It's Tanner. Oh my God it's Tanner.

I yelled with my lips tugging at my side, "WERE HERE!!"

I started speed shuffling with Greg towards Tanner.

Tanner kept yelling, "WHERE ARE YOU!?"

With my whole chest, "WERE RIGHT HERE! SCIENCE CLASSROOM-"

Before I even finished, Tanner cut the corner and started sprinting towards us. I can't help but smile seeing him. Knowing that this day is over.

I stopped moving because it felt like if I took another step, I'd collapse. I take a deep breath. Almost like I was holding my breath till I saw him.

Tanner got to us, "Miguel what the hell happened to your eye?!"

Before I could answer, I saw movement behind Tanner.

Two guys I've never seen before jogging to us. One with a thick gray beard, long hair and slim. The other one looked overweight and had a goatee. They rushed to Tanner's side.

I try to hide my shaky voice, "Tanner can you take Greg?"

The two men scrambled to Greg's side and held him up. Once they took Greg from me, I took a step back. My head felt like bricks and my vision went all blurry.

I said before I collapsed, "Tanner, I'm gonna fall."

That's the last thing I remember before my memory went blank.

October 31?

My body felt hot, but also so comfortable. My body was sinking into a cloud. Almost like I could stay here forever. I started to fall back asleep, but suddenly something cold and burning touched my eye. I flinched back and hit my head on the bedboard. The impact sent pain throughout my whole body, especially my eye.

"Damn it!"I yelled.

I brought my hand up to my eye and it's wet. I look down at my hand and there's blood.

An unfamiliar voice called out beside me, "Hey hey hey, take it easy now. I was just changing your bandage."

It was the slim old man I saw at the school. All these questions filled my head.

I blurted all the questions I had all at once, "Where am I? Who are you? What happened? Where's Tanner-?"

The man jumped in "Woah woah slow down. Your friends are in a different room right now."

I studied him for a second. His hair is in a ponytail, he has a long thin beard, and he's sitting on a stool next to the bed. I look towards myself and there's a pink and white patterned blanket over me with white sheets underneath. On top of the blanket there's a med kit near my legs. I looked back at the man and he had medical supplies in his hands.

"Can I continue?" he asked.

"Continue what?" I said, still confused.

"Before you woke up I was changing the bandage on your eye."

"What do you need me to do?"

"Just sit up for me please," he said in a calm voice.

I do just that. While I'm moving, I try not to put pressure on my left wrist because it hurts. I'll tell him about it after he's done tho not to give him too much on his plate.

He rumaged through the medical supplies.

I asked, "How's my eye?"

"Well, if you haven't noticed, you lost your eye. Your eyelid, eye, and under eye had chunks taken out." The man says while taking off my old bandage and getting a new one.

He skilfully places a wet white pad on my eye. It didn't hurt as bad as I was expecting, but it was cold. He then lifted my head from the pillow and finished wrapping the bandage around my head.

"All set," the man exclaimed. He got up with the med kit in hand and started walking towards the exit. He stopped at the door and turned towards me. "My name is Morgan, I have a family here so please be courteous around them."

I opened my mouth to say something but before I could ask for anything, he walked through the door and closed it with a click. The last thing I wanna do right now is move, so I laid back in bed. I lifted the blanket over me and looked at the window.

There's a clock in the corner of the room. It's 4:13. *How long have I been out for?* I was about to shut my eyes again but I heard footsteps walking towards my door. It swung open and revealed Tanner standing in the doorway.

Tanner rushed to my side with a concerned voice, "Hey are you alright?"

I took a second to look at myself then I turned back to Tanner, "Other than my eye and wrist, I think I'm fine."

Tanner sighed, "Damn I was scared for a while. Seeing you carry Greg with half your face covered in blood was kinda scary, but you're gonna be fine right?"

After Tanner said that, I thought about Greg's condition. The last time I saw him, his entire chest was oozing blood, and he was barely able to stand up.

I said, looking at the end of the bed, "About Greg... Please be honest with me, how is he?"

I looked back up to Tanner and he went stone faced. Tanner paused for a moment like he's trying to figure out what to say, "Greg's fine. He's staying in a different room right now. The people treating him said he needs to rest and their biggest concern is if Greg gets an infection. So I guess we just have to wait."

I felt sick, sick to my stomach, but I tried to change the subject, "Who are these people anyways?"

"The old guy that was in here, his name is Morgan. He is the owner of this house and has a wife, son and grandson living here. Morgan and Luis, his son, are the ones who got us from the school."

Tanner's voice gets heavy, "Miguel, you have to tell me what happened. How did you lose your eye and Greg get hurt that bad?"

I took a deep breath. I started the story from where we all split up.

...

After I finished. I looked back at the clock and it was 5:17.

Tanner slumped back in his chair, "So Reds dead. For sure this time?"

"Yeah. He's not coming back, thanks to Greg..." I said with a sigh of relief.

We stood in silence for a little while, keeping our heads down.

"But..." I continued, "I can't shake the feeling Red let it happen."

"What do you mean?" Tanner asked.

"I mean, Red was way more powerful then the time we fought him at the mall, he was stronger, faster, smarter. When he was about to get hit by Greg he just... turned around and stood there? Didn't bring up his hands or anything.

Tanner tilted his head, "So... Red just let himself get killed?"

Hearing him say it out loud, it did seem a little crazy, "I mean, yeah?"

Tanner scoffed, "Why would he let himself die?"

I started to feel like I did when I was talking about the man on the roof, "I don't know I just... I can't shake the feeling he wanted to lose or something?"

Tanner slightly shook his head side to side looking at the ground, "No, You beat him fair and square." Tanner looked up, "You both beat him. You're overthinking it."

*I tried to believe him, I wanted to believe him. I nod to Tanner like I understand, but I'm still not convinced. Red could have easily killed Greg if he wanted to. So why didn't he?*

Tanner got up from his chair and left the room, "Goodnight Miguel"

"Goodnight" I called back.

Tanner closed the door leaving me alone with my thoughts. Even though my muscles were tired and I had one eye permanently shut. I kept tossing and turning all night.

# Chapter 14: Left to Die

Date: 11/1/26

The air was tense in the living room. Morgan and Luis were standing next to the tv staring right at me. Tanner was getting Greg from his room. The big clock next to the couch kept ticking methodically. *What do they want to talk about?* It felt like getting called to the principal's office without knowing what you did. I can't help but question what we did wrong.

I heard slow footsteps in the hallway before Tanner and Greg came into view. Greg looked worse than what Tanner told me. I stood up, not believing my eyes(eye).

Tanner had his arm around Greg while walking. Greg's entire face is pale with no color, his eyes are droopy. Dirty bandages cover the majority of his chest and stomach. My friend is hurt. Hurt bad. I see it. I see that he's hurt, it doesn't feel real. Like this is some dream or just some crazy nightmare.

"Greg..."

Morgan cleared his throat loudly and all our heads turned towards him, "I'd rather not have him here." Morgan then lifts his finger towards Greg.

I don't know what's happening, but I didn't intervene, and with that, Greg groaned and walked back to his room.

The room door clicked and Morgan started talking, "I'm worried about your friend."

"Aren't we all?" I said like it's obvious.

"Your friend has 3 slashes and a stab wound around his stomach and chest, I don't know how to say this but...." He then pauses for a moment before he continues. "He's probably gonna die. He's probablsdfy gonna haze and infecstion asndif si maosdt slikely nkto goanas make izt."

*Gregs gonna die?*

"And ifd have atoe keapp mauy familsaudfe."

*No, I don't believe it.*

"Isamfo sosrrry asdfbut I hvasdsde tsot sdo thisa."

*What? What are you saying? It doesn't make sense.*

*"Dfor msydf famsidltys ssagftly i dshadve to kick Greg out"*

...

"What?" I looked up from the couch, "What did you just say?"

Morgan cleared his throat again, "This is a family decision and we think Greg has to go. You and Tanner seem fine but your friend is looking... zombie-like."

I'm completely taken aback, "He's zombie like? Did you find a bite mark?"

"Well no but-"

I stood up, "Then he's not turning into a zombie!" I raised my voice higher than I should have.

Morgan backed up with wide eyes, "And how do you know that!?" He barked, "I have to take care of my family right now. I don't know how people are turning the way they are but I'm not gonna chance it."

My head began to burn hot, "So you're just gonna throw my friend under the bus? Because you're scared?" I stepped towards Morgan with my fist unknowingly clenched.

Luis, from the front of the room, pulls out something from behind his back. He then held a shotgun firmly in his hands, slightly pointed at my legs.

Morgan yelled, "Luis slow down!" Morgan turned back to me "Im sorry about-"

I cut him off, "Forget it. If you weren't gonna accept Greg here then we might as well leave anyway."

I stormed towards Greg's room.

Luis yelled at me going down the hallway. "Be Grateful! If not for us you'd be dead!"

I opened Greg's door and slammed it behind myself.

"Greg, get ready we're leaving."

Gregs sitting on the side of the bed, "Yeah, I heard."

Tanner opened the door quietly and shut it behind him, "Miguel, what the hell was that?"

"The hell was what?"

"Why did you get so mad!?"

My head was starting to burn, "Why aren't you mad? They are asking us to kick Greg out!"

"But could we have reached an agreement or something?"

I looked at Tanner in the eyes, "Well... they pulled a gun on me. So it's a little too late for that now, huh."

There was a silence between all of us for a few moments before I continued packing. All of us started to grab our belongings and put them in our bags. After a few minutes we collected all our items. Greg couldn't carry a backpack so me and Tanner divided his stuff into both of our bags and left some stuff we didn't need.

We all put our gear on. I put my axes on my belt and Tanner grabbed his katana. I found a black beanie on top of a drawer. I put it over my head to cover the bandages. We walked out of the room with me carrying Greg, and Tanner leading the way. We passed the living room with Morgan and Luis silently watching us. Tanner held the front door for us and we left the house.

A cool breeze hit us in the face as soon as we were outside. All I saw was a forested road with a lot of green and orange-colored trees. We walked towards the road and stopped.

I asked, "Where exactly are we?"

Tanner said, "We are on the east side of town. In the country a lil bit. If we go right we can make it back to town."

I adjust Greg's arm on my shoulder, "Let's go back then."

Greg said coldly while taking his arm off my shoulder, "I can walk by myself." Greg grunted and started walking down the road.

...

The next hour of walking was silent. No one said a word. Occasionally we would point out a zombie and either me or Tanner would kill it. Finally, we saw a familiar building in the distance.

All of the sudden, Greg asked, "Do you guys hear that?"

I took a second to listen for something, but I heard nothing but the wind, "What are you talking about?"

"That... whispering," Greg said.

I got goosebumps by what he said, "Dude, don't joke about stuff like that."

Tanner added, "Yeah it's probably just leaves or something."

Greg said in defeat, "Yeah, you guys are probably right."

*If only we **listened,** maybe we could have done something about it...*

# Chapter 15: Dead End

Date 11/1/26

Tanner said, "We should go to the hospital for Greg."

"Yeah, I think that's a good idea."

...

We were walking on the sidewalk. There were buildings on each side of the road. The air was cold but the sun was cooking my skin. While I'm taking in the breeze, I heard something. Walking, stomping, groaning.

I whispered, "Guys" I walked to the corner of the building on my left. I could hear Tanner and Greg follow closely behind. I peeked the corner and I saw it. Horde of zombies. All jumbled up on the street. I quickly took my head back so the zombies had no chance to see me.

I turned to my friends, keeping my voice low, "We have to go another way."

...

After a while, we made it to the front of the hospital with a half full parking lot. Can't imagine how many zombies will be in there, but at least the hospital has everything we need.

The Hospital is 3 stories tall. The structure is pretty much just a big block. The last time I had to go there was when I needed my blood drawn. There's a big open area at the entrance that leads to long hallways and stairs.

We walked up to the entrance and the doors and windows were made of somewhat transparent glass. The window had a white fog to it. I grabbed the handle and pulled it open. Immediately an arm launched from the gape of the door.

I tried to slam the door shut but the zombie's body was in the way.

"Kill it! Kill it! I yelled.

The zombie tried to reach his arm around the door to scratch me. He smacked me in the face first then I ducked but kept pressing the door with my back. Tanner has his katana firmly in hand. He brought it up and struck the zombie's head with a strong crunch. The zombie's head squirted on me and around. Some on Tanner. The body then went limp, stuck in the door. After a moment of silence I pushed off the ground and turned around. The body fell into its own pool of blood on the pavement.

I looked at the group and Greg had a hand on his head, "After all this time it's still gross."

"Let's just go." Tanner said tired.

I grabbed the handle and opened the door. We walked in and there's another set of doors to open. After that, we entered the lobby. It's a small, open area. Yellow sunlight would shine through the windows. The floor was a pool of blue and white. But there's blood. A lot of blood. Down the hallways that lead to black.

I turned my head to the counter. There's a zombie with its mouth open and looking towards us and it kept bumping into the counter. He had a gaping hole in its neck and had a bite taken out of its cheek. No open wounds. No flesh showing. Just dried blood covered the sides of its body.

"Miguel come on," Tanner said softly.

Greg and Tanner are going down the dark hallway, "Let's go!"

"Right, ok" I said back.

I walked over and we all pulled out our flashlights from our bags. I pointed a beam down the hallway and I saw two balls of light look back at me. Then 4 then 6.

*Damn it.*

"Greg, light up the area" I commanded.

Tanner puts away his flashlight and unsheathes his katana. I took out my axes with my hands trembling. *Kill the zombies, all you gotta do.*

There's screeching down the hallway. The balls of lights started to rapidly get closer. In no time the lights showed their bodies.

The closest one gets sliced in the neck by Tanner. Another zombie sprints my way. I step up and slam one of my axes in his left arm. The zombie screamed and with its mouth open, I slid my ax through its lips leaving its head barely attached.

I looked up and Tanner's katana was stuck in the zombie's head. I ran over and grabbed the butt end of the katana and pulled out. It got unstuck and we both fell back a bit. I looked back up and a zombie immediately got right on me, battering my jacket. I pushed it to the left with my axes in hand.

Its head and body jolted around. His head went up. Then back down, but its eyes didn't stay on me. He sprinted towards the left. I tried to get in the way but I'm too **slow.**

The zombie lunged towards Greg. It pinned him against a pillar. I heard a thump, then Greg fell down. I rushed over. The zombie battered Greg with its hands. I wrapped my right arm around the zombie's neck and pulled with my legs. I pushed with everything I had and I fell onto my back.

I looked over to Tanner, still hold the zombie, "TANNER HELP ME"

"GIVE ME A SECOND!" Tanner yelled back.

He's killing a zombie. The zombie frantically squirms around in my arms. I wrapped my legs around the zombie's waist and pulled harder. I pulled up, I squeezed my legs, bent my back until I heard a tear and crack from the zombie neck. It went limp and I pushed it to the right, making him roll.

I picked up my axes from the ground and stood up quickly. I'm breathing heavily, headache, my muscles are tight, but there's no more zombies. Tanner pulled out his katana from the last one's head. I looked around ready to strike for what felt like an eternity, but Greg's groans brought me back.

"Greg!" I rushed over to him and squatted down. "Yo yo yo, are you ok?"

He's doubled over holding his stomach again.

"Hold on buddy let me see." I grabbed his jacket zipper and pulled down slowly. When I got to the bottom my head got steaming hot. His white shirt. It's stained in bright red blood.

*No no no*

"Greg can you stand?"

He started wheezing and said nonsense, "*Your can't be real...*"

I raised my voice, "Tanner common, COME HERE!"

I stood up and grabbed Greg's left arm. Tanner rushed over and grabbed the other. I said, trying to keep my voice calm, "Let's go Greg" We lifted Greg up and I gave him to Tanner. I bent over and picked up both my axes that were on the floor. I put one in its sheath and the other in my right hand. I reached into my pocket and grabbed my flashlight. "Let's go."

I lit up the way and we walked down the hall. Then made a left. We entered the first room that we saw. When I walked in, I rushed to the counters looking inside them. Tanner and Greg walked in together, locking the door behind them. I look through one cabinet I started with the top,

Alcohol, yes

Gauze, Yes

Bandage, no

Pills, no

Staples, no

Cleanex, no.

I put alcohol and gauze onto a table and continue searching frantically. Scissors, no No, No yes, Yes, No,Yes. I put everything I thought I needed and some more onto a table next to the sink.

I turned to Greg, sitting in a chair holding his stomach. Tanner put a lantern on top of the patient bed so we could all see in the room. I put all the supplies on a chair next to Greg's.

I said looking at Greg, "Ok, uhh stand up?"

Tanner put his hand on my shoulder and nudged me back, "Miguel, Let me do this, I know what I'm doing."

I snarked back, "I know what I'm doing!?"

"Miguel, let me do this right now." Tanner then turned his back towards me to treat Greg.

I reluctantly grabbed a rolling chair to sit down. My arms are resting on my knees. My right leg can't stop shaking. *Greg's fine, I know he is. So why am I shaking? Why is my head burning hot?*

Suddenly I heard a muffled rumbling. Almost exactly like the rumbling at Greg's house. I stood up and left the room.

A voice called out from the lobby, "What the hell happened here?"

I tip tow to the corner and peeked my head around the corner. Men. A lot of men. 6-7 people. They have helmets on and a lot of gear.

An old guy with a raspy voice, "You see this one? His head is chopped off from the mouth." He said in disgust.

One guy took out a pistol from his hip, "These bodies are still bleeding. Whoever did this is still here." After he said that he flipped on a flashlight and beamed it down the hallway I was in. The light hit my eye and I pulled my head back.

"Shit, down there" One of the men said.

I rushed back to Greg's room and shut the door behind me

I whispered, "We have to leave."

A deep voice called from the lobby, "We're not here to hurt you! Just come out with your hands up!"

Greg is wrapped up and is putting his jacket back on. I helped pick him up and we walked out the room. Tanner carried his left side and I carried his right. We walked left, away from the lobby. There is an exit sign all the way down.

Tanner said, “Greg we gotta go.”

Just then light hit our backs, “HEY DROP YOUR WEAPON!"

We all stop moving.

I whispered to Greg and Tanner, "There's a stairway to our left.”

I let go of Greg and turned around.

“HEY! I SAID DONT MOVE!” The man yelled.

All I can see is the light and a gun above pointed at me. From behind me, I heard Tanner slam the stairway door open. I ran to the right and shoved Greg and Tanner into the stairwell.

A gunshot, BANG!

I shut the door behind us and use my body to stop the door, “TANNER GO!”

Tanner ran with Greg in his arms up the stairs. “GO” I yelled again. Then the men started to bang on the door. I pushed harder with my legs but one of the men eventually got an arm through the door.

I took my ax from its holster and held it in my hand. I thought of something to give Greg a little bit more time. The first time I used my ax on a person. I bring my ax up and slam it into the arm poking through the door.

The connection made a sickening thud and his arm snapped halfway up his forearm. With blood pouring out. He screamed and violently pulled back. All he did was rip his own arm off his body.

"AAAAAHHHHHH" His arm dropped to the ground next to me. The door closed and I stood up and ran up the stairs. The door behind me burst open and men started to spill out into the stairwell. I made a turn and ran up the next step of the stairs. I go up another set of stairs and see Greg and Tanner. I passed them to open the stairwell door. They walk through and I close it behind us.

"Let's go Greg! We have to go!"

Greg said weakly, "I'm tired."

I'm starting to drag Greg down the hallway, "Just a little bit more."

"I'm tired," Greg repeated.

"Greg just-"

"I'm tired!" Greg yelled.

Greg took his arm off me and Tanner. He walked to a patient's room and swung the door open. Tanner and I rushed into the room watching Greg. He walked to the end of the room and sat on the floor under a window.

I quickly go to Greg's side, "Greg what are you doing! We have to go!"

"I can't!" Greg yelled at me. "I can't this time... I can feel it."

"What... what are you talking about?"

Greg started panting, "I feel like I'm dying Miguel."

"Greg please dont say that, please dont. You're just tired..."

Tanner ran to Greg's side after he locked the door, "What are you talking about?"

Greg's eyes started to water, "I feel like I'm gonna die. I don't want to die."

Tears start flowing from my face, "And you're not. Just hang on! You'll feel better soon. Just take a lil break."

"It hurts." Greg's voice shakes and his lips switch. "Please, I don't wanna hurt."

Tanner whimpered, "Greg I-I-I"

Greg started to touch his necklace, He took it off and placed it in his bloody hand. "Miguel... take it."

"What" I said between sobs.

"Take it... please. For me"

I grabbed his hand with both of mine, "I'll take it."

"Stay friends. Ok." He sniffled, "Please?"

"We will Greg we will" I repeated.

Greg's arm went limp in my hands.

"Greg? Greg? Say something." Tanner pleaded.

"Greg?"

"Greg!?"

*Greg please, dont go.*

His eyes went blank. His mouth hangs open. His head rested on his shoulder, and then his eyes closed shut.

I cried, "No no no. Please don't be gone, I can't lose you too. Greg, please don't go."

Loud footsteps echo through the hallways, "Open The door!"

The banging on the doors was drowned out by my head. This is the one time I didn't over think, one time my leg stopped shaking, ONE TIME I didn't do anything.

Just me. My heart beat, and Greg, laying there asleep. With his eyes closed. All I could see, all I could feel.

Never reached 16

Never finished school

Never had a girlfriend

Hell, never even held hands with one. But when he wakes up, I'll get him a girl, we'll get to celebrate his birthday. And we'll do it with Tanner.

"Right Greg? Right..."

The banging on the door got louder and louder. But I didn't move an inch, why would I? I cried into my hands. An ugly cry. Cried and cried.

"Miguel"

Cried

Tanner's voice called out, "Miguel... look"

I wiped my eyes and looked up. I see Greg's legs. I jumped backwards. "Greg?" He was standing straight up with his eyes closed.

Tanner said with a smile, "Don't do that shit! Were you joking!?"

He reaches for his shoes and pulls out his metal pipe. He then opened his eyes. Red. Glowing dark red. "So soon..." Greg said, shaking his head.

"Greg?" I questioned

He looked down at me and Tanner, "I know you?"

Suddenly the door behind us burst open, with the armed men rushing in, weapons drawn. While I had my attention on the armed men, the sound of shattered glass erupted behind me. I turned around and the window was shattered with no sign of Greg. *What should I do? What can I do?* I don't know what to think anymore. Too much to think and my mind goes blank.

"Miguel! stand up we have to fight!"

Shattered glass all over the floor.

"GET AWAY FROM US!"

"Kid calm down, we're not here to hurt you."

The walls are white

"We will shoot you if we have to!"

It's chilly in the room

Im cold

# Chapter 16: Trapped

Date: 11/1/26?

I'm in a cell of some sort. From little I remember, they put me and Tanner in a car and drove us somewhere. I wasn't paying attention to the details. Next thing I know I'm in a room with a window too high to reach. A dusty room made of concrete. A single bed with a plain sheet. Without my backpack. *Who took us? Where am I? Why didn't they just kill me? Where's Tanner?*

***What's*** Greg?

So many questions but I don't have the energy to deal with it. I've been in this room for hours now. Trying to do anything to keep my mind occupied. Thankfully I keep my journal in my jacket. So I can write the final events up to my boredom. There was so much to do before. Now, I'm just laying in bed until something happens.

# *Authors note*

Wow, that took a long time. I started the book when I was 12 and stood on a rocky mountain until I finished at the age of 15. I gotta first thank my entire family that read my book and gave me pointers on what they liked and didn't like. Then I gotta thank my dad for helping me edit the small things I missed while writing the book, and my friend Truman Duffy editing the first couple of chapters. I can't thank them enough for letting me ramble my ideas to them and share my thoughts. The characters and setting is centered around my life so a lot of the characters are people around me, like my brother Mathew and my friends.

Writing this book feels like creating my own universe that anything I say goes. It's a very unique feeling that I came to really enjoy. One thing that I had a problem with at the start was creating unique characters. It was really hard for me and I had to sit for a day to think about who I wanted in the book. I eventually decided to base it on my life, friends, and family.

The story about Miguel and his friend is one that I enjoy deeply. I wanted the story to feel raw and genuine. Something that would actually happen in a zombie apocalypse scenario. With characters having contracting beliefs and viewpoints of the apocalypse and zombies. I also wanted the story to be realistic. I never liked stories being over the top gory just to be so. I like to keep everything like it would be in real life. No one's invincible. No one's the main character. Just a kid writing in a journal.

After that cliffhanger, I'm not gonna end the story there. I'm gonna make another continuation of the story in the near future. I want to create more stories for people to read so expect to see more from me. If you're reading this, you're the best and thank you for reading my book.

***Thank you!***

Kathi S. Barton is an award-winning and bestselling author known for her steamy paranormal romances and unforgettable characters. A recipient of the prestigious Pinnacle Book Achievement Award, her books have topped the charts on Amazon and All Romance eBooks, earning her a loyal global readership.

Kathi lives in Nashport, Ohio, with her husband, Paul. When she's not crafting passionate love stories set in magical worlds, she enjoys camping, exploring local auctions, and attending county fairs, where Paul showcases his artwork and pottery. Her creative spark—fueled by a muse she describes as a cross between Jimmy Stewart and Hugh Jackman—brings her stories to vivid, heartfelt life.

Paranormal romance with plenty of heat is her favorite genre, and she loves connecting with her readers. Feel free to reach out—Kathi would love to hear from you.

Email: aaronskiss@gmail.com

Follow Kathi on her blog: http://kathisbartonauthor.blogspot.com/

www.ingramcontent.com/pod-product-compliance
Lightning Source LLC
LaVergne TN
LVHW090515110826
845146LV00003B/870

*9798891265349*